Look for these titles by *Maya Banks*

Now Available:

Seducing Simon
Colters' Woman
Understood
Overheard
Undenied
Love Me, Still
Into the Mist
Stay With Me
Reckless

Coming Soon:

Into the Lair
The Cowboys' Mistress

Brazen

Maya Banks

A Samhain Publishing, Ltd. publication.

Samhain Publishing, Ltd.
577 Mulberry Street, Suite 1520
Macon, GA 31201
www.samhainpublishing.com

Brazen
Copyright © 2008 by Maya Banks
Print ISBN: 978-1-59998-814-6
Digital ISBN: 1-59998-564-0

Editing by Jennifer Miller
Cover by Anne Cain

First Samhain Publishing, Ltd. electronic publication: September 2007
First Samhain Publishing, Ltd. print publication: July 2008

Dedication

To "Mom" because I think you're too cool. My request for adoption was real, by the way.

Chapter One

Jasmine Quinn stared at the email message in her inbox and smiled as she read the text.

Of course you can come home. And about damn time, too. We've missed you, Jaz. You shouldn't even feel you had to ask. I've already booked your flight into Houston. Your confirmation numbers are below. I'll meet you at the airport.

—Zane

Home. She stood up from her desk and shut the laptop before moving to the window overlooking the beautiful Parisian skyline. In the distance, the Eiffel Tower gleamed and twinkled with a thousand lights.

She loved it here, and she'd miss it, but she loved it back home on the Texas ranch more. Even if she hadn't considered that she'd return when she left a year ago. She stepped out onto her small balcony, and breathed deeply as the late spring air blew over her face.

Zane and Seth. She couldn't wait to see them. It had been painful to stay away from them for the last year. So many times she'd nearly caved, picked up the phone and asked to come back home. But going back to a place where she'd be reminded of her feelings for both men on a daily basis and having to cope with never having a chance with either had made going back impossible. Until now.

Now? She was going back with a purpose.

When she arrived in Paris, she'd been defeated. Heartbroken and convinced she'd never get over the painful dilemma she left behind. Cherisse had changed her outlook, changed so many things about Jasmine's way of thinking. It was because of Cherisse that Jasmine was taking a chance.

She wouldn't go home the same little girl Zane and Seth had looked out for after that disastrous night in Houston so many years ago. A light shudder worked over her shoulders as she revisited her past shame.

No, she'd go home a sophisticated, mature woman. One who knew what she wanted and exactly what she had to do to get it. After a year away, Zane and Seth would see beyond their overprotective tendencies and see *her*. A living, breathing woman with adult needs. She needed them. She needed what they could give her. And somehow she knew that they needed her just as much.

໖

Jasmine reached back to unclip her hair, letting it fall around her shoulders. She dragged her fingers through the strands and tucked the layered bangs behind her ears as she stood waiting for the line of passengers in front of her to disembark. She twitched with impatience and tapped her foot accordingly.

She shoved her thumbs into her jeans pockets and looked down at the waistband that barely cleared the top of her pelvis. The shirt she'd chosen to wear bared a three-inch strip of her abdomen and teasingly bared more when she moved her arms upward.

Yeah, she'd chosen her outfit carefully. She wanted to knock Zane's socks off. It would help to get a reaction from him before she had to face Seth at the ranch. Seth was going to be a harder sell, of that she had no doubt.

He was the oldest, the responsible brother. Zane was the younger, more laid-back sibling. He'd flirted shamelessly with her in the past, but it had never gone beyond idle teasing. She was going to change that come hell or high water.

Finally the line moved and she surged ahead, anxious to see Zane after so long. She strode up the long ramp and finally burst into the terminal. She didn't waste any time. She skirted around the people milling about and headed for the security checkpoint where she knew Zane would be waiting.

As she traveled down the small exit corridor, anticipation quickened her stride. When she stepped out of the hallway, she stopped and stared around, her heart beating an anxious rhythm. Then she saw him.

She sucked in her breath and tried to control the urge to run pell-mell and throw herself into his arms. She drank in the sight of him. A curl of heat untwisted in her stomach, fanning out until she felt warm all over. If she thought she was attracted to him before, the reality of seeing him for the first time in a year hit her square in the hormones.

He stood staring at her, a smile carved into his handsome face. He hadn't changed a damn bit.

His midnight black hair fell to his shoulders, a slight curl making it unruly. A diamond stud glinted in his left ear. He wore a tight T-shirt that stretched across bulging biceps and a hard, muscled chest. Wrapped around his upper arm, between the upper and lower muscle, was an intricately woven tattoo. A pair of deer antlers interrupted the circular flow of the band. It was the same graphic that was branded into the metal arch over the driveway to Sweetwater Ranch.

Zane's blue eyes twinkled in welcome, and when he opened his arms, she forgot all about not throwing herself at him. She felt the sting of tears at her lids. She was home. She flew across the crowded room and launched herself at him.

He caught her with a chuckle and palmed her ass as she wrapped her legs around his waist.

"Gee, Jaz, one would think you missed me."

Following her instincts, and her desire, she ignored his outburst and pressed her lips to his. He stiffened in surprise, his hands tightening on her behind.

For the briefest of moments he returned her kiss, allowing his mouth to work hot over hers. It was a bolt to her system, a welcome flood of desire.

One of his hands slid up her back, resting against her spine. She shivered at the feel of his palm against her bare skin. His tongue brushed over the curve of her mouth before he tore his lips away. He stared at her, his eyes wide with shock and something else. Lust. He blinked rapidly and eased her body down his until her feet hit the floor with a thud.

Behind him, the sound of a throat clearing caught her attention.

It was then that she saw him. Seth. Standing behind his brother. Had he been there the whole time? Why hadn't she seen him before now?

A groan worked from her stomach into her throat. She hadn't known he was coming. Zane hadn't told her.

She swallowed and looked up at him, her mouth gone dry from the hard frown he gave her. He closely resembled Zane. He still wore his hair cut short, but it was the same silky black as his brother's. His eyes were the same intense blue, and the tattoo on his arm was an exact match to Zane's. But she knew Seth wouldn't be caught dead with any piercings.

Where Zane gave the appearance of being easygoing and laid back, Seth was his polar opposite—ultra responsible and brooding, seriousness etched into every facet of his face.

"Hello, Seth," she said nervously.

He looked curiously between her and Zane. It didn't help that Zane shuffled from foot to foot and wore an expression that screamed "guilty as hell".

"Ah, why don't we go see about your luggage, Jaz?" Zane asked.

"Do I get a hug?" she asked Seth in a husky voice.

He hesitated for a split second before opening his arms to her. She walked into his chest, curling her arms around his waist. She buried her nose in his shirt and closed her eyes.

This was coming home. For a year, she'd ached for him. Missed him. Yearned to be back home and in his arms. And finally she was here.

A current of electricity flowed between them, something that had been absent in the past. She could feel his quick intake of breath, as if his realization of her was sudden and unexpected.

After a second, his hand crept up to stroke her hair. He kissed the top of her head. "I missed you, little bit."

It was something he'd called her plenty of times in the past, but now it irritated her.

She pulled away, frowning at him. "Little bit?"

He grinned. "You're still a little bit of a thing. You barely reach my chest."

She clenched her teeth together in annoyance. He was already putting distance between them. Already labeling her as the little girl he was used to. Maybe it made him more comfortable, but she didn't give a damn about his comfort. She wanted him to burn the way she burned. Want the way she wanted.

She turned to Zane, easing her jaw as she smiled at him. "Let's go get my luggage. I can't wait to get home."

"We're not immediately going home," Seth said.

She shot him a sideways glance. "No?"

He shook his head. "I've reserved hotel rooms for us. It's too late to start back now. You're no doubt tired from your flight. We can go home in the morning."

She nodded then quickened her step to catch up with Zane. He slid an arm around her shoulders as she leaned into him.

"I missed you, Jaz," Zane said. "It's damn quiet at the ranch without you."

She elbowed him in the side.

"You've sure grown up, little girl," he continued. His eyes raked up and down her body.

She suppressed a smug grin. Yeah, he'd noticed. She'd bet anything he was still reeling from the kiss she'd given him.

"Well, I can't stay a little kid forever," she said lightly.

Beside her, Seth frowned. She shot him a questioning stare, but he looked away.

They approached the carousel where her luggage was going to be. A large crowd of people lined the conveyor belt as the bags started to spill out the end. Seth laid his fingers on her arm.

"Wait here. Zane and I will get your stuff."

She watched as the two men pushed through the crowd until they came to a stop beside the carousel. Women and men alike stared at them. They were arresting characters, wild and formidable looking. In the beginning, she'd spent a lot of time staring at them too, never sure whether they were the good guys or the bad.

They had a confident, self-assured look that they wore like a second skin. It bordered on arrogance, but Seth wasn't so much arrogant as he was convinced.

Her stomach tightened in appreciation when Zane bent over to read the luggage tag on one of her suitcases. His jeans pulled across his ass, molding to every contour. The denim encased thick, muscular thighs. When he stood up again and lifted her suitcase over the side, the muscles in his arms bulged and rippled the thin T-shirt he wore.

Ten minutes and several suitcases later, both men returned to where she was standing.

"Damn, Jaz, I don't remember you bringing this much shit with you to Paris," Zane complained.

She laughed. "That's because I bought most of it while I was there. Here, I'll take some of them."

"We'll get them," Seth said.

She looked up at him, and for a moment, their gazes locked. She didn't try to hide the hunger she knew must be reflected in her stare. Fire briefly flamed in Seth's eyes before he turned away.

"Let's go," he muttered.

After piling all her luggage into Seth's extra cab truck, they got in and navigated to I-10 West. Thirty minutes later, they pulled into the parking lot of a hotel, and Seth hopped out to check them in.

Zane and Jasmine got out, and Zane piled as much of her luggage as he could fit into the cab of the truck. She snagged an overnight case with the things she'd need for their hotel stay then walked into the hotel behind Zane.

As they approached the desk, Seth turned around, holding two envelopes containing keys.

"I booked two rooms. They're adjoining."

He handed Jasmine her key.

Jasmine followed the two men to the elevator, still staring at the card in her hand. Separate rooms, huh. When they'd seen her off to Paris a year before, he hadn't concerned himself with getting her a separate room. He'd booked a suite.

They got off the elevator and walked several feet down the hallway before Seth stopped and dug for his key. She looked at her own envelope for her room number and moved a few steps past them to the next door.

"See you in the morning," Seth said as his gaze followed her.

She smiled and gave a small wave before entering her room. She shut the door behind her and tossed her bag aside. Dismissed and not even home for an hour yet. On one hand, she supposed it was better that he hadn't booked one room. He obviously saw her as a threat to the way things had always been between them. Which meant he recognized her as a desirable woman and not a child.

"Or maybe he just doesn't want to see you make a fool of yourself," she muttered as she flopped down on the bed.

She'd give them fifteen minutes, and then she was going in. She changed into one of Seth's old football shirts she'd taken with her to Paris. It was modest enough, hanging to her knees. She didn't want to be blatant. Subtlety would get her a lot further. If the imprint of her nipples could be seen through the shirt, oh well. She wasn't going to sleep in a bra.

Checking her watch, she walked over to the adjoining door and knocked softly. When Zane opened it, standing there in just his jeans, she nearly swallowed her tongue. Lordy but the man had a chest that made her want to slobber.

She breezed past him, not giving him a chance to object to her being there. She sat on one of the beds with a slight bounce and looked over at Zane.

"It's kind of lonely over there. I haven't seen you guys in a year."

Zane smiled and sauntered back over to the bed. "Want to watch some TV with us for a while?"

She beamed back at him and promptly pulled back the covers and curled underneath.

A few seconds later, the bathroom door opened, and Seth strode out with just a towel around his waist. As much as she wanted to pretend indifference, as much as she'd have loved to look away and play it cool, her eyes traveled up his body until they rested on his hard abdomen. The towel dangled precariously low. Just a half inch lower and she'd get a peek of the dark hair she knew resided there.

Seth looked up and uttered a surprised oath when he saw her lying in the bed.

"Jesus Christ, Zane, you should have told me she was in here."

He hauled the towel up higher and stalked back into the bathroom.

She raised wide, innocent eyes to Zane. "What's his problem?"

"Turn your head, Jaz, let me get into my shorts," Zane directed, ignoring her question.

She sighed and turned her face away. Seconds later, the bed dipped, and Zane crawled up beside her. He reclined, propping his elbow on the pillow next to her.

"Now suppose you tell me what's going on in that pretty little head of yours," he drawled.

She gave him her best confused look. "I missed you guys," she said huskily. "You didn't miss me?"

He arched an eyebrow at her, and she watched the battle play across his face. He was clearly trying to decide if she was playing a game or if she was just being the same girl they always knew.

"Of course we did," he soothed.

"You don't act like it," she muttered. "What's up Seth's ass anyway?"

He opened his mouth to speak then shut it again. Finally he shook his head. "Come here, Jaz," he said.

She didn't hesitate. She rolled over and scooted her back into his chest until she was snuggled into his arms. As his warmth bled through her skin, she sighed in contentment.

"Glad to be home?"

She nodded. "I loved Paris, but I was ready to come back home to Texas."

She sighed again when his fingers tangled in her hair, gently pulling downward as he brushed the strands.

The bathroom door opened, and Seth came out again, this time fully clothed. He frowned when he saw Jasmine hugged up tight against Zane. She pretended to ignore him, focusing instead on the TV.

He seemed to battle over whether or not to object to her presence. She watched from the corner of her eye as he looked at her. With a slight shake of his head, he walked over to his bed.

Feeling like she'd won this round, she smiled to herself and burrowed deeper under the covers. She was tired. Exhausted, actually. But she didn't want to spend her first night back alone.

She could feel Zane's heartbeat against her back, and it soothed her. Made her feel safe. It felt like home.

As she wiggled closer into the shelter of his body, her behind brushed against the vee of his legs. For a moment, she paused. Then she felt the hardness against the curve of her ass.

Zane must have registered her awareness, because he jerked away and rolled out of the bed. She felt the loss of their closeness keenly and, for the first time, regretted the attraction between them.

Zane strode into the bathroom and closed the door behind him with a bang.

Chapter Two

Seth watched Jasmine's eyes close as she succumbed to sleep. His brother still remained in the bathroom after his exit over fifteen minutes ago.

She was beautiful. Achingly so. It shamed him that he couldn't look at her without feeling a surge of lust. He ran a hand through his hair and stood up, a weary sigh escaping him. He yanked back his covers and picked the remote up to turn off the TV.

What the hell was he going to do? He reclined on the bed, leaving the blankets at his feet. The year she'd been away had been a blessing and a curse all rolled into one.

He'd missed her. Missed everything about her. But at the same time, he'd been relieved not to have to face her on a daily basis.

He looked up to see Zane walk cautiously out of the bathroom. His brother shot a look at the bed and relaxed when he saw Jasmine sleeping.

"What the fuck is wrong with you?" Seth demanded in a low tone.

"Nothing," Zane growled.

Seth raised an eyebrow.

Zane sighed and sat on the edge of Seth's bed.

"I can't touch her without getting a hard-on," he admitted.

"Then don't fucking touch her," Seth said, anger spilling into his voice. He swallowed then lowered his voice so as not to wake Jasmine. "I mean what did you expect? You were practically on top of her in the bed. She isn't a little girl anymore, Zane. That shit's got to stop."

Zane's eyes glittered with irritation. "I don't need a goddamn lecture from you. Do you have any idea how hard it is not to touch her when she's constantly close to me, hugging me, snuggling? Jesus. It wasn't like this before she left. I never had a problem with her affection, and I damn sure don't want to hurt her feelings now. How the hell is she supposed to understand what's going on? It's not her fault she's turned into a drop-dead gorgeous woman that I can't even look at without wanting to fuck."

Seth surged forward, his fists clenched. "Shut the hell up, Zane." His harsh whisper exploded over the room and both men looked over at Jasmine. Seth leaned in closer to his brother. "I'm warning you. Cool it. And stay the hell away from her. We didn't bring her home to be our fuck toy. She is strictly off-limits."

Zane looked at him, a mixture of hurt and surprise in his blue eyes. "Is that what you think of me? You think I'd disrespect her like that? Hell, Seth, we've been taking care of her for six years. Do you honestly think I'd do anything to hurt her?"

Seth blew out his breath in frustration. No way he'd admit to having the same difficulties around Jasmine. No way he'd tell Zane that within hours of her return, he was already struggling with the same dark thoughts that had plagued him for years.

"No, man, I don't think anything like that. I know you love her. We both love her. Which is why we're going to stay the fuck away from her. It's our job to take care of her and see that she's happy."

"Agreed," Zane said. But even as his brother spoke, he glanced sideways at Jasmine, and Seth could see the raw hunger in his eyes.

Fuck. He could feel it too. It ate at him, but his hunger had gone on a lot longer. Now that she was back, he was on fire. The days ahead were going to be the most difficult he'd ever face.

"Let's get some sleep," Seth said wearily. "We've got a long drive tomorrow. Maybe you should take her room."

"Yeah," Zane muttered as he got up.

He disappeared into the adjoining room, leaving Seth to stare over at Jasmine's sleeping form. Her dark brown, nearly black hair spilled over the pillow, and her body moved with her soft breathing. She'd grown out of her gawky girl's figure and developed the curves and swells of a lush woman. But she'd always been beautiful to him. Even when she was all arms and legs and wide green eyes.

He itched to trail his finger down her cheek. He wanted to taste her lips, wanted to know if she tasted as sweet as she looked.

His jaw clenched until his teeth ached. He was such a sorry bastard. He'd sworn never to touch Jasmine. Not after the way she'd come to him and Zane in the first place. He couldn't take her down that path again. She was too young, and she needed them to take care of her. Not fuck her.

He rolled away so he no longer stared at her. He reached back for the light switch by the bed and bathed the room in darkness. Morning couldn't come soon enough.

৪০

Zane stepped into the adjoining room, his gaze traveling first to Seth's empty bed and then to the bed Jaz had slept in. Jesus. He almost retreated into the other room again.

She lay on the bed, still sound asleep, but the covers tangled at her feet, her bare legs stretched out over the bed. The old football shirt she wore had ridden up her thighs until he could see the lace of her underwear.

He shut his eyes and groaned. Hell's bells. Jaz wasn't supposed to come home all grown up and exotic. Fuck. She hadn't looked this way when she'd left, had she? Surely he would have noticed. Lord knew she'd spent enough time wrapped around him.

They were tight, him and Jaz. He'd always been her shoulder to cry on. She'd spent more than one night snuggled up in his bed when her past had come back to haunt her in a big way. But never, *never* had he reacted to her sexually.

Now all of a sudden he was one big fucking hormone, and his dick had taken over for his brains. Jesus. He felt fucking betrayed. He loved that little girl, and he damned sure didn't want to be lusting after her like all the guys he'd threatened to kill over the years.

He started guiltily when the bathroom door opened and Seth walked out. His older brother eyed him curiously before walking over to throw his toiletries in his suitcase.

"We should be getting on the road," Seth said. "I'd like to be home as early as possible. Carmen is expecting us, and if I know her, she's cooked enough to feed an army for Jasmine's homecoming."

Zane nodded and swallowed. "I'll wake Jaz up."

He walked over to the bed, purposely keeping his eyes as far from the bare expanse of her legs as possible.

"I'll do it," Seth interjected, shoving in front of Zane. "You get the luggage down to the truck."

Zane frowned in irritation. "Don't fucking treat me like I'm some kind of goddamned rapist, Seth. I was honest with you, which is more than I can say you were with me. But that doesn't mean I'm going to jump her bones at the first opportunity. Now get out of the way so I can get her up."

Seth put his hands up in surrender and turned away. Zane shook his head and sat down on the edge of the bed next to Jaz. He reached out to touch her hair. He let his fingers trail down the strands until he reached her shoulder. He shook her gently.

"Jaz, wake up, honey. It's time to go home."

She didn't so much as flinch. He smiled and shook her again.

"Come on, sleepyhead. Up and at 'em."

She stirred, and her eyes fluttered open, a sleepy, dreamy look to them. She stared up at him then smiled, and his chest lurched.

"Good morning," she whispered.

He leaned down to kiss her forehead, just like he'd done a million times in the past. Only now he felt cheated. He wanted to explore her lips.

"Get up, Jaz. We're heading home. Carmen's waiting for you."

She struggled to sit up, and he eased off the bed. He stood for a second, not really knowing what to do to alleviate the tension he felt. Then he walked over and snagged the two suitcases Seth had just zipped up.

"I'll take them down," he said shortly. "I'll meet the two of you in the lobby."

Jasmine watched him go, a mixture of hurt and confusion wracking her brain. Was he avoiding her now? This wasn't something she'd counted on. She knew it would be difficult for them to see her in a new light, but had it been all too easy? Were they no longer comfortable around her as a result?

She wasn't ready to let go of the relationship she shared with the two men who had taken care of her for the last six years. She loved them, wanted more than their protection. She wanted their love. Oh, she knew they loved her, but she wanted the all-consuming love. The kind between a man and a woman, not the kind they'd given a sixteen-year-old runaway from the streets.

She looked up at Seth who regarded her cautiously. The wariness in his eyes wasn't something she was used to. He'd never been easy, but he'd always been hers. Her friend and confidant. Her protector. She didn't like the distance that had opened between them in the space of a few hours.

"Is something wrong?" she asked softly.

He shook his head and looked away.

She looked down, trying to control the wash of emotion his rejection caused. The Seth she knew would never have turned away from her like he just had. It hurt.

Across the room, she heard Seth groan. Then suddenly he was in front of her, pulling her into his arms.

"I'm sorry, little bit."

The endearment did little to comfort her. She looked up at him. "Should I have stayed in Paris?" She held her breath, praying that he really hadn't wanted that. If he didn't want her...she hadn't given consideration to that possibility. What if he was tired of being responsible for her?

25

He bit out a curse and clasped her face between his hands. "Look at me, Jasmine. You will always have a home here. Do you understand me?"

She studied him for a long moment, searching his eyes for something, though for what, she wasn't certain. "But do you want me here?"

"Of course I want you. I can't believe you'd have to ask. Honey, I don't know what's going on with you, but never doubt that you are welcome at the ranch. It's your home. That won't change. You understand that?"

She leaned forward, his hands still framing her face, until her forehead rested against his. She put her arms around his neck in a hug. "I've missed you, Seth. I only feel at home when I'm with you and Zane."

He sat there a minute longer then slowly stood up, letting his hands fall from her cheeks. "Zane's waiting on us. Go on and get dressed. I'm going to head down to the lobby to check out. Come down when you're ready."

ഇ

The miles stretched out over the West Texas landscape. Flat, barren, but beautiful to her. Jasmine stared out the window as the truck ate up the highway. The sun was high overhead, and although it was just the end of May, the heat had already settled in.

She leaned her forehead against the glass, idly listening to the two men talk in the front of the truck. Her mind was occupied with memories of the first time she'd taken this trip. A scared sixteen-year-old. No clue what the future held. Desperate to be away from the circumstances of her past.

She closed her eyes, remembering that night in a Houston bar when she'd approached Seth, her throat nearly swollen shut in fear. She'd propositioned him, knowing her only other choice was to be tossed back onto the streets. When he flatly refused her, she'd panicked, knowing he was her last chance.

He'd demanded to know how old she was as Zane watched in horror. They both looked disgusted at how she was dressed and the fact she'd offered herself for sex. She told Seth she was nineteen. He called her a liar and demanded the truth.

It was only when she saw the man standing across the room watching her, the man who'd insisted she earn her keep starting that night, that she'd broken down, sobbing in earnest as Seth and Zane stared at her in stunned silence.

The brothers had flanked her, all but dragging her out of the bar. They drove to a nearby café, sat her down, made her eat and demanded the whole truth.

She confessed that she'd run away from home and ended up on the Houston streets. No money, no way to eat or support herself. She'd been picked up by a ruthless pimp and expected to earn her keep by prostituting herself. Only she'd failed miserably. That night had been her final chance, and Seth had turned her down flat.

After that, there hadn't been any question. The brothers drove her straight home to their ranch, hired Carmen as a housekeeper/chaperone/mother figure and they'd never looked back.

And so began her life at the Sweetwater Ranch.

To avoid any awkward questions as to why they were harboring a minor, they'd hired a tutor for her, and she'd finished high school at the ranch. After taking her GED, she'd enrolled in online college courses. Life at the ranch had been good, even if somewhat isolated. Bouts of loneliness and restlessness had led her to get into trouble on occasion. She grinned as she remembered all the times she'd snuck out to Tucker's bar only for J.T. Summers, the local sheriff and longtime friend of Seth and Zane, to haul her back to the ranch.

"You're quiet back there, little bit."

She looked up to see Seth staring at her in the rearview mirror. She smiled. "Just drinking in the scenery," she said. "After a year in Paris, it's like seeing it all again for the first time."

"We'll be there soon," Zane said. "You've been off in your own world back there. Did you even realize we're just a few miles from the ranch?"

She sat up straighter to examine the landmarks, a spark of excitement shooting up her spine. Sure enough, they were a short distance to the ten-thousand-acre spread that housed the Sweetwater Ranch.

"Is Old Man still prowling around?" she asked as she leaned forward between the two brothers.

Zane chuckled. "Yeah, the old bastard is still alive and kicking. He must be six years old now. Last season he sported fourteen points. I'd love to have him scored by Boones and Crockett."

"You're not going to kill him!" she exclaimed.

He chuckled. "No, sweet thang, we're not going to kill your pet. We want him to mate as many does as possible. He's got great genes. Precisely the kind of deer we want a reputation for at Sweetwater."

"Did you guys have a good season last year?"

"Yeah," Seth broke in. "Managed a few record-book harvests. Happy customers. A few returning hunters. About all we can ask for."

She leaned forward eagerly as they turned into the long, winding road that led to the ranch. They passed under a wrought-iron arch that bore the name of the ranch as well as the intricate design that mirrored the tattoos on Seth's and Zane's arms. As they pulled up, an older Mexican woman ran from the house, her arms waving madly. Jasmine smiled and piled out of her door.

"*Mi niña, mi niña!*" Carmen exclaimed as she swept Jasmine into her arms. "You are home at last. I've missed you terribly, *mi niña.*"

Jasmine gave herself over to the firm hug of the woman who'd been mother and nurturer since Jasmine's arrival at the ranch all those years ago.

"I've missed you too, *mamacita.*"

"Can you still speak Spanish, eh *niña*? Or have you been among the French for too long now?"

"*Sí, mamacita,*" she said with a smile.

"*Bueno, niña!* Now come, come. Let the boys bring your stuff inside. We have much talking to do. You must tell me all about Paris. Oh, and did the boys tell you, tomorrow we are having a fiesta, a celebration to welcome you home. I have been cooking all week, *niña.* All your favorites."

Jasmine let herself be pulled inside, a happy smile on her face. She'd missed home so much in the last year. Missed the way Carmen mothered her like an overprotective hen. She always seemed to know exactly what Jasmine needed, and right now, she could really use a mother.

Chapter Three

Jasmine ran a finger underneath the thin bikini strap at her hip to smooth the line as she traipsed down the stairs. Carmen's fiestas always involved lots of food and a pool party. While Jasmine wouldn't get into the water if her life depended on it, she'd sunbathe and watch the guys horse around.

J.T. was already here, along with Kyle Richards and Toby March. Her bedroom overlooked the patio, and she'd peeked out her window to see them all playing in the pool. Only Seth hadn't made an appearance yet.

She made a pass through the kitchen to see Carmen on her way to the patio. When Carmen looked up and saw her, she immediately began babbling a stream of Spanish.

Jasmine laughed. "What's wrong with my bikini, *mamacita*?"

Carmen glared at her. "That is no bikini, *chica*. That, that," she sputtered. "That's just a string draped around your private parts. Ai yi yi, are you trying to drive the boys crazy, *niña*?"

"Just two of them, *mamacita*."

Carmen threw up her hands and continued to mutter. She attacked the bread dough she was kneading with ferocity. "You're playing with fire, *niña*. Mark my words. What's come over you? You didn't used to parade around in skimpy outfits trying to drive my boys crazy."

30

Jasmine wrapped her arms around Carmen and hugged her tight. "I love them, *mamacita.* I've always loved them. But they'll always look at me like a little girl unless I do something to make them notice me."

Carmen dropped the dough and wiped her flour-covered hands on her apron before returning Jasmine's hug. "You be careful, *mi niña.* I love you like you were my own daughter. I don't want to see you hurt. If you tease those boys, you have to be prepared for the result. That's all I'm saying, eh? You be careful."

Jasmine smiled. "I will, *mamacita.* I promise." She hugged Carmen again. "I'm so glad to be home."

Carmen clucked and shooed her away. "I'm glad you're home too. Now go on and have fun. This is your fiesta. I'll bring out some more food in a while. If I know those boys, there's nothing left."

Jasmine grinned and hurried for the patio. She paused inside the glass doors, gathering her courage to go out. Carmen was right about one thing. You could hardly call the strings of her bathing suit an actual bikini. Other than a thin triangle covering the curls between her legs, the rest of the suit was a series of strings. One around her waist and one resting in the crack of her ass. And her top. Well, it covered her nipples, and that was about all she'd say for it.

With a fortifying breath, she opened the sliding doors and walked out into the sun. The concrete patio felt warm underneath her bare feet as she padded toward the lounge chairs lining the pool.

A series of whistles rent the air, and her cheeks grew tight and warm. She glanced sideways to see the men staring at her from the pool. She couldn't look away, despite the fact she was mildly embarrassed. Four hot men slicked down with water, droplets beading and running down hard chests. Damn.

She swallowed as her gaze found Zane. Her mouth went dry. His wild, black hair hung limply to his shoulders. The sun glinted off his wet skin, drawing attention to the bulging muscles. His earring winked at her in the light.

"Jesus, Jasmine, when did you go and grow up on me?" J.T. yelled out as he made his way to the side of the pool.

She smiled and waved then continued on to the chair a few feet away.

"Come on in," Toby called out, gesturing for her to jump in.

She shook her head, a cold sweat beading on her forehead at the thought of plunging into the ten-foot-deep pool. "I'm just sunbathing."

She settled into her chair and began rubbing suntan lotion over the front of her body. She moved with slow, sensuous motions and watched from the corner of her eye.

Zane watched her, but then so did the others. She wasn't normally such an exhibitionist, but the attention gave her a tiny thrill.

Finally she reclined, closing her eyes to soak up the warmth of the sun's rays. In the distance she could hear splashing, the men's voices.

Sometime later, she felt cold droplets on her stomach. She opened her eyes to see Zane standing over her, water dripping from his hair. He stared down at her, his gaze lowering to her stomach.

"You know Seth is going to shit a brick when he sees that, Jaz."

She arched an eyebrow then looked down at her belly ring. She fiddled with the thin gold loop with her fingers. "You don't think he'll like it?" she asked innocently.

Zane chuckled. "You know damn well it'll make him crazy. He'll blame it all on me and call me a bad influence."

"Do *you* like it?" she asked, staring back at him.

Zane swallowed and looked away. "It looks great on you. Uh, when did you get it done?"

He was uncomfortable, that much was obvious. She smiled a little. "In Paris. I missed you. Getting the piercing reminded me of you," she said softly.

His eyes flew back to hers, fire building in their depths. Before he could respond, she rolled slowly onto her stomach.

"Could you untie my top and rub some suntan oil on my back? I don't want a tan line," she said.

She heard his swift intake of breath. Felt his eyes on her naked skin. His hands shook as he gingerly untied the strings and let them fall beside her.

It was all she could do not to moan in pleasure when his big hands rubbed gently over her. He smoothed oil over her shoulders, down to the small of her back. She held her breath. Would he touch her ass? God please let him touch her.

She closed her eyes when his hand closed over one cheek and then the other. He spent less time there, hurriedly applying the oil before standing back up.

"Thank you," she mumbled, her face still hidden in her arms.

She heard him walk away then heard the splash as he jumped into the pool. His touch still lingered on her skin. Still burned hotter than the sun shining down on her.

As the sun rose higher, she drifted languidly between sleep and waking. She tuned out distant sounds as she floated. Then suddenly, the sun was blocked from her body. A shadow fell over her.

She pried one eye open and looked in the direction of the obstruction to see Seth standing over her, a dangerous glitter in his eyes.

"What the fuck are you doing, Jasmine?" He spread a towel over her ass before she could respond. "Since when do you lie around in the buff to sunbathe?"

"I'm not naked," she mumbled.

He reached down to retie her straps. When he was finished, she rolled back over. She put a hand to her eyes to shield the sunlight as she stared up at him.

"See?" she challenged. "I'm dressed."

"If you call that dressed," he said darkly. "And what the hell's up with the belly ring? Did Zane talk you into that?"

A hoot of laughter rose from the pool.

"See, I told you he'd blame me," Zane called.

"You don't like it?" she asked Seth.

"For God's sake, Jasmine, you didn't used to cavort around half naked or put unnecessary holes in your body."

She worked to keep the amusement from her face. "I'm not a little girl anymore, Seth. I'm all grown up. You can't expect me to look like a sixteen-year-old forever."

It was the wrong thing to say, and they both knew it. He sobered, and she looked away, embarrassed by the memories conjured for both of them.

"Just get some clothes on," he said gruffly. "Here." He stripped off his T-shirt and tossed it to her. "Put that on. You're going to get burned if you're not careful."

She watched as he walked to the far end of the pool where Carmen had set up a table with snacks and drinks. The horseplay resumed in the pool, and she wondered just how much of their conversation the others had heard.

She was about to toss aside Seth's shirt and ignore his dictate when Toby pulled himself over the side of the pool and headed in her direction.

Instead of stopping to talk to her as she expected, he simply reached down and plucked her out of her chair. He grinned wickedly.

"Time to come in," he said.

She immediately began to struggle. "No!"

He obviously thought she was playing because he ignored the panic in her voice and started to sprint back to the pool. She writhed in his arms, desperate to make him stop. Her chest began to close in on her, swelling with the god-awful fear she'd lived with for so long.

She heard a shout in the distance. Saw Seth start for her, but he'd never reach them in time. Everything moved in slow motion. She registered Zane thrusting a hand out, trying to stop Toby. Heard Seth's snarl of rage.

Oh God, not this, not the water. She whimpered as Toby jumped into the air. They seemed suspended for a moment, and then they hit the water, his arms still tight around her.

As the water consumed her, closed over her head, she began to fight. It was her worst fear all over again. The man shoving her underwater, terrorizing her, holding her under until she nearly passed out only to yank her above water and start all over again.

They sank to the bottom, Toby still holding her. He had no idea of her fear and why should he? Her chest felt near to exploding. Darkness swirled around her. She gave one more effort to free herself, to somehow shove herself to the surface. To escape the nightmare.

Just when she knew she was going to black out, strong hands wrapped around her waist and pulled her upward. Zane. They broke the surface, and she clutched desperately at his neck. She heard desperate sobbing and realized it was her making the terrible noise.

"Shhh, baby, you're okay now," Zane whispered in her ear as she choked and cried, coughing up water.

He held her tightly against him as she buried her face in his neck. She trembled from head to toe, panic quaking over her.

Zane eased through the water, swimming with her in his arms as she clung to his chest. When he reached the side, another set of strong arms lifted her up and out of the water.

"Jasmine, honey, are you okay?" Seth asked in her ear as he cradled her dripping body to his.

She wrapped her arms around his neck and cried harder. He tensed against her, anger billowing from him. He strode around the pool toward the patio doors. In the distance, she heard Zane issue a sharp reprimand.

"Don't you *ever* fucking touch her again, you got me?"

Then she heard no more as Seth closed the doors behind him. The air-conditioned air blew over her, raising goose bumps on her skin. She shivered against him, whether more in fright or cold she wasn't sure.

He took her upstairs to her room. Once inside he set her down, holding on to her as she got her feet underneath her.

"Stay right here, baby. I'll be right back with a towel."

She shook like a leaf, clutching her body with her arms. Tears streamed down her cheeks. She couldn't get rid of the awful tension in her chest. It still felt as though she couldn't breathe. She sucked in air, trying to ease the ache.

Seth returned and wrapped a warm, fluffy towel around her. Then he scooped her up in his arms and carried her to the bed. He set her down, taking care not to jostle her. She sat there, the end of the towel gathered in her hands, held tightly, her lifeline.

"Jasmine," Seth said gently. "Honey, talk to me. Are you all right? I'm so damned sorry that happened to you. I swear I'm going to kick Toby's ass."

She opened her mouth to try and tell him she was okay, but she wasn't. Another sob escaped her chest, followed by another and another.

Seth cursed under his breath and took her in his arms, holding her tightly as he rocked back and forth. Behind him, the door burst open. A few seconds later, she heard Carmen and Zane asking about her.

Seth continued to rock her even as he asked Carmen for a sedative. Jasmine buried her face in his thickly corded neck. She felt such a fool. It had been years since she'd needed the tranquilizers the doctor had prescribed for her panic attacks.

A warm hand soothed over her back, and the bed dipped behind her as Zane sat down. He pressed a kiss to the back of her head and kneaded her shoulders as she lay against Seth's chest.

"I'm so sorry, Jaz. I never meant for that to happen."

She hiccupped softly under Seth's ear. She felt so safe here, between the two men who'd taken care of her. It was the only place she felt free from the terror of her past.

She inhaled Seth's scent, drawing comfort from his strength.

Slowly, with great care, Seth pulled her away until he could look her in the eye. His hand caressed her cheek and cupped her chin, holding it as he examined her. Behind her, Zane continued to stroke her back until her muscles began to relax.

"Jasmine, it's been a lot of years, honey. Don't you think it's time to tell us why you're so afraid of the water?"

Chapter Four

Jasmine stiffened as dread crawled over her shoulders and took firm hold around her throat. As much as Seth and Zane knew about the circumstances of her past, she hadn't told them everything. They already knew too much.

Shame crowded her already cluttered mind, and she tried to look away, but Seth's fingers remained firm around her chin.

"Jaz," Zane said softly.

Seth loosened his hold, and Jasmine turned slightly so she could see Zane. His blue eyes were tender with understanding.

Zane touched her cheek with one finger. "You don't have to tell us anything you don't want to, but you need to understand that nothing you say will make us think any less of you."

She tried to smile, but her eyes went all watery again.

"Here, *mi niña*," Carmen said as she entered the room carrying a glass of water. "I have your pill."

As Seth took the glass of water, Carmen made shooing motions with her hands. "You boys go on now. Let me take care of Jasmine. She needs rest after such an upset. I'll put her to bed."

Seth handed Jasmine the glass of water and reluctantly rose from his perch on the bed. Zane kissed the top of her head and also stood. He slid a hand over her shoulder and squeezed comfortingly before he and Seth walked to the doorway.

She stared after them as they left before Carmen stepped in front of her and urged her to take the sedative. Jasmine stared at the tiny pill for a long moment, suddenly angry.

She curled her fingers until they formed a tight fist around the sedative, and then she looked up at Carmen.

"I don't want it, Carmen."

Carmen's face softened in sympathy. "There is no shame in taking it, *niña*. You've done so well for so long."

"Which is why I don't want it now," Jasmine said. "I can't—I can't keep freaking out over something that happened so many years ago."

Carmen wrapped her arms around Jasmine and hugged tight. She stroked Jasmine's hair and made soothing, motherly noises, the kind that made Jasmine close her eyes and absorb the hug like a junkie desperate for a fix.

"I'm very proud of you, *niña*. You're a good girl, and you've come a long way from that frightened child those boys brought home six years ago."

Jasmine smiled against Carmen's chest. "I love you, *mamacita*."

Carmen pulled away and smiled down at Jasmine. "And I love you, *niña*. You are no less my daughter than if I had given birth to you myself. All I lack are the stretch marks. Now, in to bed with you. You need rest. You're still not up to snuff from your trip."

Jasmine allowed Carmen to fuss over her as she got changed into an oversized T-shirt. Then she crawled into bed, and Carmen pulled the covers up to her neck and dropped an affectionate kiss on her forehead.

"Sleep tight, *niña*. If you need anything just call for me, okay?"

Jasmine smiled and nodded. As Carmen left the room, Jasmine allowed the sleepy tug of her eyelids to take over. She turned and hugged her pillow tight against her chest, willing herself to relax and give in to the numbness of sleep.

ಬಿ

Jasmine woke in a cold sweat. The cool air from the vent above her bed blew over her damp skin, and she shivered. For a moment, she regretted not taking the sedative. Her sleep had been fractured by frightening images. Dark memories. Even now, wide awake, the knot of fear in her throat refused to abate.

Someone had left the light on in her bathroom and the door ajar so that a faint glow shone into her bedroom. As she glanced to the window, she saw that night had long since fallen.

Her ears picked up no noise within the house. Only the faint sounds of the night outside her window could be heard.

Another shiver took over her body. She didn't want to be alone.

She gave no second thought to her decision as she swung her legs over the side of the bed. Her nightshirt fell down her hips to mid-thigh as she stood. She eased from her room and padded down the hallway to Zane's.

She frowned when she saw his closed door and wondered for a moment if she should go in or not. He'd never slept with it closed before. In fact, he'd always left it open on purpose in case she came in during the night.

She laid her palm over the wood and stood for a moment before finally twisting the knob with her other hand. The room was dark, but as she opened the door wider, the light from down the hall illuminated it enough that she could see Zane in his bed.

Silently, she moved forward, blinking to adjust to the dim light. As she got to the edge of the bed, she could see Zane was naked, the sheets tangled at his feet.

He was asleep on his back, one arm over his head, tucked beneath his pillow. The other arm rested across his abdomen. Her gaze dropped lower. As soon as it came to rest on his groin, she looked guiltily away.

She wasn't here for some madcap seduction. The thought hadn't even crossed her mind. She shouldn't have come at all. It would only make things more awkward than they already were.

She turned away, biting her lip to squelch the betraying quiver.

"Jaz?" Zane's sleepy voice reached her, and she froze.

She turned back around, careful to keep her gaze in a neutral location. "I'm sorry," she said. "I'll go."

Zane looked down as if just realizing he was naked. He swore and yanked the sheets up to his waist. She turned around again and started to walk to the door.

"No, don't go, Jaz. Give me a minute, okay?"

She stopped, gripped by indecision. She heard him scramble out of bed, and when she peeked around, she saw him pulling on a pair of shorts. When he was done, he reached over and turned on the small lamp by his bed. Then he walked over to her and put a hand on her arm.

"What's wrong, Jaz?"

She felt pretty stupid when it came down to it. She'd been gone for a year, and before that, it had been months since she'd last come to his room in the middle of the night. Of course he wouldn't have expected her to come barging in. She hadn't thought beyond her need for comfort, something he'd given her more times than she could count.

"I shouldn't have come," she said quietly. "I didn't think."

Zane pulled her toward the bed. He put both hands on her shoulders and pushed her down until she sat on the mattress. Then he sat down beside her.

"Of course you should have come," he chided. "*I* didn't think. I should have realized that after what happened, you'd have trouble sleeping. Is there anything I can get you?"

She looked over at him. How could she tell him what she most needed? "I just didn't want to be alone," she said.

He moved over until he was on the other side of the bed. He shoved the covers down then patted the spot beside him. She hesitated for a brief moment before crawling up beside him. She positioned herself so she faced away from him.

He reached down, pulled the covers up and wrapped one arm around her waist. When she snuggled back against his chest, he pulled away so that a small space separated them. She regretted the distance immediately. She knew why he'd done it, and instead of thrilling her as it might have under other circumstances, his awareness of her reinforced the breach that was opening up between them. A breach that she wasn't altogether sure she could overcome.

"I'm sorry I wasn't able to stop Toby," he said. "I've made damn sure it won't happen again, though."

"It's not your fault I'm such a fucked-up mess."

"Turn over," he commanded as he pulled at her waist.

Surprised, she shifted and rolled her body until they faced each other. He stared intently at her, and suddenly she wished he hadn't turned the lamp on. It was much easier in the dark when he couldn't see her.

"I know we don't talk about what happened six years ago, and maybe that's not a good thing. I think our silence has sent the wrong messages, made you think we're ashamed of you in some way."

When she opened her mouth to speak, he silenced her with a finger to her lips.

"Seth and I don't talk about it because we don't want to make you uncomfortable. I think now we might have made a mistake. Maybe we should have been talking about it a whole lot so you could get it out of your system and quit dwelling on it."

She cast her eyes downward, unable to keep staring at him.

"If you're not ready to talk about it, that's fine, but if you've got the notion Seth and I think less of you, then you need to get that out of your head quick."

Silence descended between them. She chanced another look up at him to find him studying her, his eyes soft with understanding.

"Can I sleep here?" she asked. "I—I don't want to go back to my room."

He accepted her diversion without argument. He leaned over and kissed her forehead, only he lingered a little longer than usual. She could hear the catch in his breath as he withdrew.

"I'll get the light," he said, as he rolled away abruptly.

He reached up and extinguished the light, plunging the room back into darkness. It was a moment before she could dimly make out his features from the narrow beam feeding into his doorway.

She eased over, turning her back to him once again. She wanted him to put his arm around her waist like he had before, but he didn't move. She let out a small sigh of disappointment and stared at the door.

Zane listened to her uneven breathing, knowing she wasn't close to sleep. Which was fine, because it wasn't like he was going back to sleep anytime soon.

He wanted to touch her, ached to touch her. There was nothing more he wanted to do than to hold her in his arms and tell her that it would be all right. He wanted to make love to her, to explore every curve, kiss her silky skin.

He closed his eyes, willing himself back to sleep. But his mind wasn't cooperating, and his body damn sure wasn't either. Every muscle was wound tighter than a rattlesnake ready to strike. If she'd fall asleep, then at least he could get up, take himself away from temptation.

Finally he rolled away from her, positioning himself so his back was to hers. He stared at his closet door and mentally began ticking off all the reasons why he couldn't go down this road with Jaz.

He was well into his list when he felt her turn over to face his back.

"Zane?"

He tensed. "Yes, honey?"

She hesitated for a moment. "You remember the night in the bar?"

That had his full attention. He reached up to turn the light back on then rolled back over until he faced her. She looked at him with uncertain eyes.

"I remember."

She licked her lips, and her gaze darted away from his face. He didn't move, didn't breathe. Though he and Seth were well aware of what had happened at the bar and the reasons behind it, the events leading up to it were very much a mystery. Jaz had never talked about it, and they'd never pressed her.

"The man who expected me to prostitute myself, to work for him...I didn't agree at first. I was desperate. I had no place to go. No money. No food. But the idea of selling myself to strangers for sex scared me worse than the thought of living out on the streets. So I told him no."

Zane studied her face as agony worked its way across her brow, crinkling her eyebrows and locking fear into her eyes. He wanted to reach out and erase it, tell her that nothing would ever threaten her again.

"And what did he do?" Zane prompted.

Her pupils dilated, and her breathing became more erratic. "He shoved me into a hot tub and held me under. Just when I thought I'd surely pass out, he'd pull me out, let me catch my breath, then do it all over again."

Zane closed his eyes as every single muscle in his body went rigid with anger. Goddamn, mother fucking son of a bitch!

"He wouldn't stop until I agreed to do what he wanted." Her voice caught on a quiet sob, and he felt the sound all the way to his soul. "I was such a mess, scared out of my mind, scared that I was going to die. I would have agreed to anything."

No longer able to keep from touching her, he reached across the space between them and pulled her into his arms. She buried her face in his chest, and he could feel her shudder against him.

"It's stupid, I know," she said, her voice muffled by his body.

He let her go just enough that she could breathe and he could hear her more clearly.

"I wouldn't even take baths after that. Still won't. If there's more than a few inches of water, the mere idea of it covering me..."

"You don't have to explain yourself to me, Jaz." He rubbed his hands over her back, up and down, wanting to comfort her in any way possible. "Fear is inexplicable, and I don't blame you for being terrified of the water after going through that."

"That's only part of my nightmare," she admitted.

He tugged at the strands of her hair, moving them from her face and tucking them behind her ear. "What's the other part?"

She gazed at him, eyes shining with unshed tears. Then one slipped over the rim and trickled down her cheek. He wanted to kiss it away. Wanted to kiss her eyelids. Instead, he gently thumbed the wetness away and waited for her to continue.

"Sometimes I think about what would have happened if I hadn't met you and Seth in the bar that night. If it had been someone else."

Her voice broke and the last few words came out in a shaky exhalation. She opened her mouth as if to explain further, but she swallowed and looked away again as another tear slid rapidly down her cheek.

"Oh, baby," he said around the ache in his throat.

He ignored the voice inside that warned him to keep his distance. Ignored the idea that he should have sent her back to bed as soon as she'd shown up in his room.

He ran his fingertips over her cheeks, swiping at her tears as he leaned his head in. He caught her gasp of surprise as he touched his lips to hers.

Sweet. Exotic. Liquid heat exploded between them. As much as he'd been dying to taste her since she'd kissed him in the airport, nothing had prepared him for the reality.

Her lips moved over his, seeking, opening for him. He swiped over her tongue, and his initial intent of offering comfort flew out the window as her hands crept over his stomach to his chest. This went beyond comfort. He needed, wanted, ached.

Christ.

What the hell was he doing? She trusted him. She depended on him. And all he could think about doing was peeling her shirt off and loving every inch of her delectable body.

He pulled away, sucking in several steadying breaths. He willed his pulse to settle before his heart exploded right out of his chest. He was as hard as a rock, a fact that shamed him. He tugged the covers so that his erection was disguised by the sheets and shifted to try and alleviate his growing discomfort.

"Jaz," he began, hoping like hell to divert his focus away from her swollen mouth, because it was far too easy to imagine it closed around his cock. "Did you never think about going back home?"

He wanted to recall the question. It was stupid. But it was the first thing that had popped out in his quest to cover the awkward moment. She'd told him and Seth enough that they knew home hadn't been a happy place. But surely it would have beat life on the streets?

Sadness shadowed her eyes, dulling them. "I didn't have a home anymore."

He nudged her chin upwards, wanting to open the door further into her past. "Why not?"

She sighed and rolled out of his arms onto her back. She stared up at the ceiling, a distant look to her eyes. "I told you my mom died."

Zane nodded though he doubted she saw.

"Growing up, it was just me, my mom and my older brother. He was ten years older so we weren't particularly close. I mean he looked out for me when I was a kid, but he joined the Army right out of high school. He and my mom got into a terrible argument over some guy she wanted to marry, and so he never kept in touch.

"After all that, she didn't even end up with the guy. I didn't like him either, but I know she was lonely. Then she got sick. Cancer. She died within three months of the diagnosis."

Zane's chest tightened at the sadness in Jaz's voice. "How old were you when she died?" he asked quietly.

"Fifteen."

He frowned but didn't interrupt her. She was sixteen when he and Seth had found her in the bar. What had she done in the year between her mother's death and then?

"I was sent to foster care. I hated them. They hated me. I went through three homes in a matter of weeks. The last family was a real winner. They had a twenty-year-old son, and dad and son thought it would be fun to have their own personal plaything. I left after three days."

Zane put his hand on her head, tunneling his fingers into her hair. It made him angry. So goddamn angry. What if he and Seth hadn't been the ones Jaz approached that night? Would she even be alive now? A cold chill crept over his skin at the idea of what might have happened to her.

He continued to stroke through her hair, waiting, not wanting to push her.

"You know the rest," she said dully. "I was young and stupid. Thought I could make it on my own. No place to go but no place to go back to either."

Silence settled over them. She still stared up at the ceiling, though he knew she was about as far away from here as one could get. He didn't want her hurting, didn't want those painful memories to do so much damage. He wanted to make it better, but he didn't know how.

Finally, she turned her head until she looked at him. Deep sadness registered in her gaze. "I miss her," she said simply.

"Your mom?"

She nodded. "We never had much, but she always made sure I had enough."

"I'm sorry, honey."

She smiled then and reached up to put her hand on his cheek. "I'm glad I'm home. I missed you and Seth. And Carmen."

"We missed you too."

She yawned and took her hand down from his face to stifle the sound. He seized the opportunity with both hands.

"Get some sleep, Jaz. It's been a long day."

He leaned over and kissed her forehead as if that simple gesture would replace the fact that he'd devoured her lips just moments earlier. He couldn't forget it, but he could hope she would.

She stared at him for a long moment then slowly nodded. He reached for the lamp and doused the room in darkness once more. When he turned back to her, she rolled over then promptly scooted into his chest. He nearly groaned in frustration.

"Zane?"

He sighed. "Yes, honey?"

"I love you."

The words did strange things to him. She'd said it before. She'd always been affectionate with him. But he'd never taken it seriously. He'd never had an issue with returning the words. They'd always rolled effortlessly off his lips, but now they stuck in his throat as if saying them would change the course of their entire relationship.

He curled his arm around her waist as she snuggled deeper into his embrace. She felt...right. And who the hell needed sleep anyway?

Chapter Five

Seth hauled himself out of bed even earlier than usual. It wasn't quite light yet, and he'd planned a busy day. He was supposed to meet the wildlife biologist for breakfast then take him out over the northeast quadrant to look at areas he'd selected for food plots.

He showered quickly, his mind occupied with Jasmine instead of his coming meeting. He hated what had happened to her yesterday. He didn't like to see her scared. It reminded him too much of the way he'd first seen her. Big eyes full of fear, looking every bit her sixteen years old instead of the nineteen she'd claimed. If it hadn't been so important to get her far away from Houston and the man controlling her, he would have tracked the son of a bitch down and beat the ever-loving shit out of him.

He toweled off and dressed in jeans and a T-shirt. He didn't have to leave for another half hour, but he wanted to check in on Jasmine. So far her homecoming hadn't exactly been smooth.

Her door was partway open, but then she'd never slept with it closed. He nudged it and stepped inside, his gaze seeking her bed. He frowned when he found it empty. Her bathroom light was on, but he couldn't hear any sound from inside. He walked over and hesitated outside the open door.

"Jasmine?"

When he received no answer, he peered around the door but she wasn't there either. Maybe she was downstairs in the kitchen with Carmen.

He walked out of her room and started down the hall to the stairs. When he passed Zane's room, he stopped, not sure why. His brother's door was open a few inches, so Seth put his hand out and pushed lightly. His fingers curled around the knob as he stepped inside the frame.

Jasmine lay in Zane's arms, sound asleep. Her back was curled into his chest, and Zane had a protective arm around her waist. An angry buzz began in Seth's ears. He clenched his jaw until he damn near cracked his teeth. What the fuck was Zane thinking, and more importantly, just what the hell had happened last night?

They looked like two lovers curled tight around each other. It didn't matter that Jasmine was dressed. All Seth saw was the intimacy between the two of them.

As if feeling Seth's heated glare and the rage billowing off his shoulders, Zane stirred and opened his eyes. The two brothers stared at each other, Zane's head visible over Jasmine's shoulder.

Seth jerked his thumb over his own shoulder in the direction of the door. "I want to talk to you. *Now*," he said in a low enough voice not to wake Jasmine.

Zane's eyes narrowed, but he carefully extricated himself from the bed and gently tucked the covers around Jasmine's sleeping form. She stirred for a moment, but sighed and snuggled back into her pillow.

Zane padded across the room toward Seth, not bothering to snag a T-shirt. Seth turned and walked out into the hallway, leaving Zane to follow.

As soon as they reached the stairs, Seth rounded on Zane. "What the fuck do you think you're doing?" he demanded through clenched teeth.

Zane's expression darkened, and he didn't back down an inch. "You can shove the big brother lecture right up your ass, Seth. I don't need a fucking babysitter, and I damn sure don't need you hanging out posing as my goddamn conscience."

Carmen stomped up the stairs, hands on her hips. She pinned both men with a don't-fuck-with-me stare just before she took them both to task.

"Jasmine is trying to sleep, and you boys are just outside the bedroom arguing like two-year-olds. If you must continue, then take it downstairs. Preferably outside!"

Seth sucked in an annoyed breath. "Sorry, Carmen," he said shortly. Then he pointed at Zane. "Outside. We're not finished."

"You know what? We are. I don't have a damn thing to say to you. I don't know what the fuck your problem is. I suspect I do, but that's your deal, not mine."

He turned and stalked back to his bedroom.

Seth glanced at Carmen who stared at him, a disapproving frown marring her usually warm features.

"You boys are going to drive her away," she chided. "Now is not the time to be pushing her. She's very fragile right now. She needs you both. You are both important to her."

Guilt flushed like a damn toilet through him. "You're right," he said quietly. "She doesn't need this."

Carmen nodded approvingly then turned and walked back down the stairs. Seth watched her go, helpless confusion wracking his mind.

He wasn't entirely sure why the sight of Jasmine in Zane's bed, in his arms, set him off. It wasn't as if it was something new. Jasmine had spent a lot of time in Zane's bed. If Seth was honest, he'd admit he resented Jasmine and Zane's closeness. Zane was who she turned to when she was scared and alone.

But now, that resentment was something more. It felt an awful lot like jealousy, and he did not want to go down that road. His hands trembled and he balled his fingers into fists to control the shaking.

Had last night been more than Jasmine needing comfort? Something he knew Zane had given her in the past. He knew Zane was attracted to her, but had he crossed the line?

And why did the idea bother him so damn much?

Because you want her, dumbass. You want her so bad you can't see straight and it pisses you off that she might want Zane and not you.

Now that he'd laid it out, it made sense. It was twisted. It wasn't something he even needed to entertain, but there it was, staring him in the face like an affronted lover.

He shoved his hands in his pockets and headed downstairs. As he passed the kitchen, he muttered to Carmen that he was going to his meeting with the wildlife biologist.

ം

Jasmine woke, expecting the warmth of Zane's body. But her back felt strangely cold, and the space behind her was barren. The pillow she held to her chest was a poor substitute, and she thrust it away.

Her first instinct was to burrow deeper into the covers, hold Zane's scent to her a little longer. She had no wish to get up, to face the day, but with the new day also came an unwelcome realization.

She'd made a big mistake.

Maybe she'd known it at the time. And maybe in that moment she hadn't cared as she'd sought Zane's comfort. But in reverting to a practice that was indicative of a much younger Jasmine, she'd lost any progress in her quest to make Zane and Seth see her as something other than a frightened sixteen-year-old.

With an unhappy sigh, she got out of bed and hurried back to her room. It was time for her to grow the fuck up and take control of her own destiny. Time to stop allowing her past to dictate her every action and reaction.

It was hard to convince the two men she loved that she was a woman full grown when she persisted in throwing them into the role of protectors.

She damned the meltdown of the previous day. Damned the fact that her fears still ruled her. She was only the product of her past if she allowed herself to be. She was so much more, and her year away from the ranch had proved it to her. Now all she had to do was present that woman to the world.

She knew Zane had felt the tangible connection between them last night. It went beyond their affectionate relationship that had formed over the years. She knew it. He knew it. But he'd pulled away, and rightly so.

She stepped into the shower, determined to wash away the girl she'd been for so long. Nothing could hurt her here. The only people here who had the power to hurt her were Seth and Zane, and she doubted they even knew it.

After her shower, she dressed in denim cut-off shorts and a tank top. She didn't bother with shoes and headed downstairs.

She could hear Carmen bustling around in the kitchen and knew she should go check in. Carmen would be worried.

Instead, she found herself outside on the back patio, stepping closer to the edge of the pool.

She stared into the sparkling blue water, marveling at the fact that something so beautiful and peaceful could evoke such terror.

Mesmerized by the shine of the sun reflecting off the iridescent swirls, she knelt down, gripping the concrete ledge with both hands.

Can you breathe underwater, bitch?

His laughter rang in her ears, suddenly muffled as he shoved her head underneath the water. It filled her ears, her mouth, her nose.

His hand gripped her hair and yanked upward, just when she thought her lungs would explode. She gasped for air, choking as she coughed up water.

Change your mind yet? I've got all night. One way or another, you'll do as I've told you.

Jasmine shuddered and closed her eyes to ward off the memory. Each breath came in a shallow gasp. Her chest rose and sank in rapid succession as she struggled with her panic.

Still, she forced herself to stare down into the aqua depths of the pool. She could see herself underneath the placid surface, fighting for her life. She could see the hand holding her under and hear the derisive laughter ringing in her ears.

"No more," she whispered. "No more. Never again." Her fingers dug into the side of the pool as her anger built and swelled inside her chest.

So much rage, suppressed for so many years. For so long she'd felt that maybe she'd somehow deserved it, but now she had such fury inside her. She wanted to wrap her hands around the bastard's neck. There was no telling how many young girls he'd preyed on. How many had been forced into a life of sexual slavery because of him? She'd been lucky. An odd twist of fate had thrown her into Seth and Zane's path, a fact she would be eternally grateful for, but there were others who hadn't been as lucky. Where were they now?

No tears threatened her this day. She was too damn mad. And in that fit of anger, a surge of rebellion welled up and festered like an infected sore.

She stood up, and before she could think better of her decision, she jumped into the water.

It was cold. A shock to her system. Though she'd jumped into the shallow end, her feet slid on the bottom, and she sank below the surface.

Panic hit her square in the face, and she nearly inhaled as she scrambled to get her feet back underneath her. When she finally righted herself and got her head above the water, she was gasping. Her pulse pounded, and adrenaline ripped through her system.

Every instinct screamed at her to get the hell out of the water, and for a moment, she froze, unable to process exactly how she was going to get to the steps. She couldn't seem to make her legs work. Her arms flailed ineffectively, splashing the surface like an injured seagull.

She closed her eyes and willed the terror to go away. *Get a grip.* If she could slap herself, she would, but she couldn't seem to make her arms cooperate either.

There she stood, in the middle of four feet of water, completely powerless to do anything but shiver in the breeze. She laughed at the absurdity, and then she winced at the harsh sound.

"Walk, you dumbass. Wade over to the steps," she grated out.

Her throat seemed to close in on her, reminiscent of how she felt underneath the water, lungs burning, seconds away from taking in a huge breath only to have the water rush in.

She heard a shriek. Carmen. Then she heard the pounding of footsteps. Had she left the patio door open?

"Jasmine! What the hell are you doing?" Seth demanded.

She looked up to see him charging to the side of the pool, looking as though he was going to jump in after her. She giggled. She couldn't help it. It sounded strained, thin and tinged with hysteria. But the idea of Seth jumping in to save her when she stood in four feet of water seemed ludicrous.

"Jasmine, honey, come out of the pool," he said in a more soothing tone. "Come over to the steps."

She looked down as if expecting her legs to cooperate. Her feet swam in and out of her vision as the water swirled and shimmered.

She was in the water. And she wasn't freaking out. Okay, maybe a little, but she'd done it without completely losing her sanity.

"Jasmine," he said in a firmer tone. "Honey, you need to get out of the water now."

Was he afraid she was going to throw herself into the deep end? Fat chance of that. She nearly giggled again. She didn't have a death wish.

When she looked back up at him again, he was reaching for his shirt. Was he coming in after her? She frowned, remembering her self-lecture from earlier. She didn't need saving, damn it. No, she'd saved herself this time.

She turned and forced one foot in front of the other. She heard a hiss as Seth sucked in his breath. She glanced back at him, connecting with his gaze. His worried gaze.

"I can do this," she said quietly.

The concern lessened, and his features visibly relaxed. She glanced at the steps, seemingly a mile away. Then she made herself take another step forward. The water slid easily over her skin, dragging a bit, which added another layer of panic.

But she was determined that this time she would win. She trailed her fingers through the glossy surface. Brought both hands in front of her to cup a handful of the water. She pushed upward, water streaming over her fingers as she raised her hands. She opened her hands and let the water fall with a light splash.

The water wasn't her enemy. She was.

She bit her lip and forced herself the last few feet. As she reached out to grip the rail, Seth grabbed her wrist. He hauled her out of the water and set her down on the hot concrete.

In an instant, she found herself folded in his arms. He held her so tight against his chest, that for a moment, she couldn't breathe.

"Don't ever scare me like that again," he said gruffly.

She smiled and relaxed into his arms. She'd done it. She'd survived it. It had been scary as hell, but she felt lighter. Like she'd shed an unbearable weight. Her act of defiance gave her a freedom she hadn't felt in many years.

Seth pulled her away. His jeans and T-shirt were soaked, which reminded her that she'd jumped in fully clothed. She glanced down at the thin tank top clinging to her body, outlining every curve and swell. The dark shadow of her nipples was visible, and she could feel his gaze raking up and down her chest.

"What were you thinking?" He gripped her shoulders and gave her a little shake. His fear had evidently worn off, and now anger had replaced it.

She stared unblinkingly at him. His blue eyes blazed with ill-disguised fury. And fear.

"I'm sorry if I scared you," she murmured. "But I had to do it. I'm tired of letting him win."

"*Niña!*" Carmen cried out as she hurried across the patio, a long towel billowing in her wake. "Have you gone *loco?*"

In a few quick movements, Jasmine was completely wrapped in the big towel, and Carmen just as quickly herded her back toward the sliding glass doors, clucking the entire way.

Jasmine chanced a look over her shoulder as she stepped inside. Seth was still standing there, his damp shirt clinging to his hard chest. His gaze locked with hers, and his expression became brooding.

"A new beginning," Jasmine whispered. "I can't be that little girl anymore."

"What did you say, *niña?*"

Jasmine shook her head. "Nothing, *mamacita.* Nothing at all."

"Go upstairs and get some dry clothing on. Then come back down so I can feed you."

Jasmine smiled, but obeyed. She walked to the stairs and trudged slowly up, a sense of victory flashing brightly in her mind.

Chapter Six

Seth didn't bother going up to change his clothes. They'd dry quickly. Though he was supposed to be meeting the wildlife biologist out on the north hundred, he went in search of Zane instead.

God almighty, when he'd walked into the house after his breakfast meeting and heard Carmen's shriek and then seen where Jasmine was, he'd damn near had a heart attack. He knew yesterday's incident had a profound effect on Jasmine, but now he wondered just how deeply she was wounded.

He found Zane in the utility shed gassing up the four wheelers. He didn't waste time with a greeting. He went straight to the point.

"What the fuck went on with Jasmine last night?" he demanded.

Zane stiffened and turned around, his expression glacial.

Seth held up his hand. "I don't mean physically. I want to know what happened to send her to your room. Was she upset? Did she talk to you?"

Zane folded his arms over his chest and leaned back against the four wheeler. "Why do you want to know?"

Seth related what had just happened. "She said she was tired of him winning, and I don't know what the fuck that means. But I thought you might."

Zane's hand clenched and unclenched. His entire body was tense, and anger rolled off him in waves. "Son of a bitch," he muttered.

"What?" Seth demanded.

As Seth listened to Zane recount the events of the night before, his jaw got tighter and tighter until his entire neck ached.

Zane ran a hand through his long hair and shook his head. "She really jumped in the pool?"

Seth nodded grimly. "Yeah, she did. Scared the shit out of me. She just didn't look all there. I mean she was there, in the pool, but she didn't look or act like she had a clue where she really was."

"It took a lot of guts to do what she did," Zane said quietly. "You know how terrified she is of the water."

"Yeah, I do."

They stared at each for another long moment. There was a lot unsaid, but Seth didn't want to pursue it any further. The last thing he wanted was for Jasmine to become a bone of contention between them.

"I've got to go meet Brad," Seth finally said. "I think I'll ask Jasmine if she wants to go. It might do her good to get out for a while."

Zane nodded in agreement, but he stared at Seth a little too intuitively for his comfort.

Seth strode out of the shed and headed toward the house. When he walked into the kitchen, he found Carmen hovering over Jasmine while she ate.

"I'm heading out to the north hundred to meet Brad. You want to go?" he asked.

Jasmine looked up at him, her eyes lacking the haunted shadows of earlier. They were bright and clear. Shone a luminous green.

"Do I have time to run up and get my camera?"

He nodded. "Of course. And finish eating. I'll wait."

Jasmine gulped down the remainder of her food and shoved her plate forward. She gave Carmen a quick hug then raced upstairs to retrieve her camera. Seth wasn't avoiding her entirely. Granted he used to extend regular invitations like this, and she used to tag along behind him like a lovesick puppy, but she knew he was seeing her differently. He never seemed to be so uncomfortable around her.

She got her camera bag then tugged on a pair of jeans and hiking boots that were more suited for the terrain than her shorts and flip-flops. She hurried back downstairs to find Seth waiting for her at the garage door.

"You ready?"

She smiled and nodded, a surge of excitement rushing through her veins at the idea of spending the day with him.

They climbed into his four-wheel-drive truck and headed down one of the many dirt roads that crisscrossed the ranch property.

The land was beautiful and barren. Dry. Rocky. Few trees dotted the dusty landscape, but there was plenty of scrub brush and cactus.

Sweetwater Creek was barely a trickle when they forged the nearly dry bank. After a rain, water would often overflow the banks and run angry and swollen for a few days before rapidly dissipating.

Ahead, jackrabbits, as well as a few cottontails spooked by the truck, darted back and forth over the road. As Jasmine gazed out her window, she saw a small herd of Black Bucks meandering among the brush.

She turned to Seth. "We have more now?"

He smiled and nodded. "Yeah, I'd say one or two more got out of Lark's fence this past fall. They've been breeding, and now we have a small population."

"You don't allow them to be hunted do you?"

Seth shook his head. "No. We leave them be. We've never had the desire to get into exotics, and I don't aim to start now."

Jasmine smiled. "I bet old man Lark was fit to be tied when he lost more of his herd to us."

Seth grinned back at her. It was the first time he'd looked truly relaxed around her since she'd gotten back home. "He wanted to come over with a tranquilizer gun, dart them and haul them back. I told him if I caught his ass on our property, I'd fill his hide full of lead."

Jasmine chuckled. Lark was an obstinate, pompous ass of the first order. His idea of hunting was to lead an animal blindfolded and hobbled in front of a deer stand and let the hunter blast away.

"What are you meeting Brad for?" she asked.

"I'm planting the north one hundred. Getting his advice on layout and food types. We've managed to keep our herd healthy and disease free, and I credit him with a lot of that."

"Are you booked for this fall?"

"Nearly," he said. "We have a few weeks open in the late season, but I expect they'll fill up closer to hunting season."

"Oh, look!" she exclaimed. "Stop, will you?"

Seth slammed on the brakes, fishtailing the truck as he ground to a halt. Jasmine pointed to a hilltop about a hundred yards away.

"Is that him?" she whispered. "Is that Old Man?"

Not waiting for an answer, she yanked her camera out and rolled down her window. She focused in on the deer and took a series of shots.

"Looks like him," Seth murmured. "If it's not, it might be one of his offspring. I'm hoping it's the latter. We could use more like him running around."

She zoomed in on the rack. Covered in velvet, the antlers probably had at least a twenty-two inch spread, and she counted at least fourteen points.

"He's beautiful."

She sighed in disappointment when the deer turned and disappeared over the hill. Seth pulled forward again and continued down the road.

A few minutes later, they passed through a bump gate, and Jasmine saw a truck parked on the side of the road several yards up. Brad was leaning against the grill, and when he saw them, he straightened and waved.

Seth pulled up behind Brad and parked. When Jasmine got out of the truck, Brad looked curiously at her for a moment before recognition flashed across his face.

"Jasmine Quinn! Lord have mercy, girl. You sure have grown up."

She walked forward self-consciously only to find herself yanked against a hard chest as Brad enfolded her into a huge hug.

Jasmine peeked over at Seth to see him scowling. Brad pushed her back and surveyed her from head to toe.

"When did you get back?"

She smiled at his infectious grin. Who wouldn't fall victim to his good old boy charm? Warm brown eyes peered at her from underneath the brim of his Stetson. She let her gaze filter downward over his form-fitting jeans and scuffed work boots.

"Day before yesterday," she said.

"If you're free one night soon, I'd love to take you for a beer. You can tell me all about gay Paree and civilized culture."

She giggled at his exaggeration. "I'd love to. Just give me a holler. I don't have any plans."

Seth's scowl deepened, which only made Jasmine's smile grow wider.

"Can we get to the matter at hand?" Seth asked pointedly.

"Oh, sure," Brad said, as if he'd forgotten Seth was standing there. "Show me what you had in mind for the plots, and we can discuss your planting options."

Jasmine let them walk away, and she opted to wander in the opposite direction, camera in hand. Her boots scratched across the parched ground. In the distance, dust swirled and skittered as the wind kicked up.

She took a few random landscape shots as she simply reveled in the joy of being home. The sun warmed her to her bones, and she enjoyed the heat scraping across her cheeks.

She climbed up a slight rise and gazed down at the winding creek bank that carved through the layers of rock and soil. Two hawks circled high overhead, dipping then soaring higher.

There was a wildness to the land that called to her. Untamed, sometimes harsh, but always beautiful. It was rough and unyielding, and yet it teemed with life.

She could still remember the first time she'd seen it. Really seen it. At sixteen, she'd viewed the vast acreage as the ultimate freedom. Here she could come and for miles be the only person around. She'd spent many an hour perched on a rock, knees drawn to her chest, merely experiencing the peace she so desperately needed.

And now she was home. A year away had only made home that much sweeter. She wouldn't leave again. Not when everything she loved was right here, nestled in the beauty of Southwest Texas.

She continued snapping pictures as she topped another hill. It wasn't until she heard Seth's shout that she realized she'd wandered so far. She turned in the direction of his voice and saw him waving in the distance.

Tucking her camera under her arm, she started back. Seth leaned against the side of the truck watching her approach. She saw no sign of Brad. He must have left already.

"Get some good shots?" Seth asked as she got to the truck.

She smiled and nodded.

"Ready to head back or do you want to stay awhile?"

She looked at her watch. "I suppose we should head back. Carmen will be upset if we miss lunch."

They climbed in and Jasmine put her camera away.

"I liked the pictures you emailed from Paris," Seth said as they drove back toward the house. "I could tell you enjoyed yourself."

"Paris is fantastic. But it's not home."

He glanced sideways at her. "You missed it here."

"I missed you and Zane," she said pointedly.

He gripped the steering wheel a little tighter and looked away. He seemed uncomfortable with her statement. But that was fine. She hadn't imagined it would be easy to overcome the image he'd formed of her. It wouldn't happen overnight, but it *would* happen if she had her way.

"Jasmine..."

Her gaze found his and she cocked her head in question.

"This morning. What happened?"

Chapter Seven

Seth knew full well what had taken place after talking to Zane earlier, but for some inexplicable reason, he wanted Jasmine to trust him enough to open up to him. Like she'd opened up to Zane.

And though he'd already heard the story from Zane, as Jasmine retold it, it had a much more profound effect. He felt every twinge of fear in her voice. Felt her shame. Lived through her terror with her.

At some point, he reached across the seat and curled his fingers tightly around hers. There was a quiet, unemotional quality to her voice as she finished. It was as if the telling had numbed her.

She glanced at him from underneath her lashes, a small look filled with nervousness. It was in that moment he knew she'd feared telling him, feared his reaction. Had his avoidance of her past led her to believe he was somehow ashamed of her?

That moment in the Houston bar six years ago had always been a source of awkwardness. Neither was comfortable broaching the subject, and he'd let it lie because he hadn't wanted to bring up painful memories.

He braked and stopped in the middle of the road. He sat there a moment, Jasmine's hand still enfolded in his. Then he turned in his seat to face her.

"Why didn't you tell me before?"

"It's not something I was very proud of," she said in a low voice. "The way we met was bad enough. I didn't have any desire for you to know what had happened before."

"And what changed your mind?" He started to mention the fact that she'd only told Zane the night before, but he didn't want to betray Zane's confidence.

She shrugged. "Maybe it's time I grew up. Stop letting the past dictate my present. Maybe it's time I stopped being ashamed of something that I couldn't control. Yes, I made mistakes and I paid for them. I don't want to pay for them any longer. I'm tired of you and Zane looking at me like a child who needs protecting. So maybe it's time I started taking care of myself."

Her shoulders stiffened, and she sat up a little straighter as she stared challengingly at him.

"I don't see you as a child," he said mildly.

She arched a brow. "No? Maybe you see me as a woman, but you fight that tooth and nail. You *want* to see me as a child, so the fact that you don't isn't very consoling."

He hated when women started talking in riddles. There wasn't a man alive who could decipher what she'd just said.

"So you're saying I don't see you as a child, but I want to see you as a child, and you don't like that."

"Do you deny it?"

"Yes. No. Hell, I don't know what the crap you're saying, so I have no idea how to answer."

She slid over the seat until she was inches from his face. "It's a very simple thing," she whispered. "Either you still see me as that helpless sixteen-year-old you saved six years ago, or you see me as a woman. What do you think when you look at me?"

If that wasn't a fucking loaded question he didn't know what was. She was too damn close, and his body was betraying him in the worst way.

He averted his gaze from her eyes, but it fell to the soft mounds of her breasts, just peeking over the top of her tank top. He jerked his head back up. A child? Fuck, he wished he could envision a child when he looked at her. Maybe then his body wouldn't seize. Wouldn't tighten as if someone had clamped a vise grip around him.

"Maybe you need help deciding?"

He started to shake his head, but she feathered her fingertips over his jaw and pressed her lips to his. Shock exploded through his system. No matter how often he may have fantasized about kissing her, the reality was startling. He hadn't imagined it ever happening, because he was determined it wouldn't. Only now she'd taken the choice from him.

Her lips slid sensuously over his. Hot. Lusty. Her tongue found his in his moment of surprise. For a brief moment, he allowed himself to get lost in her sweetness, allowed himself to imagine taking her home to his bed.

He yanked away, breathing hard as he tried to settle his raging arousal. "Christ, Jasmine! We can't be doing this."

"Why not?" she challenged. "You don't want me?"

He swore. "I think we've both established that wanting you is not the issue here."

"Then what is?"

He chanced a look at her. Hurt reflected in her beautiful eyes. And something else. The faint light of determination.

"You need to forget this ever happened," he said. "We can't go down this road, Jasmine."

"Will you forget? Can you forget it?"

"I don't have a choice," he said grimly.

"Why?"

He ground his teeth in frustration. And he knew he was being an ass before the words ever came out of his mouth, but he spoke without thinking.

"Look, don't read anything into my reaction to you. You're a beautiful woman. A man tends to trip all over himself when a beautiful woman throws herself at him. But it doesn't mean anything. It could have been any woman."

Her swift intake of breath was like a rifle shot. Hurt spilled into her eyes even as her lips tightened in anger. He braced himself for her response, but she said nothing. She grabbed her camera bag and turned to the door.

"Jasmine, wait," he called as she opened her door and jerkily got out.

She put her hand up without turning around. "I can make it back by myself."

"Don't be stupid," he began. "It's three miles back to the house."

She turned then, eyes blazing. "I said I'll make it back by myself."

Seth swore and hit the steering wheel with his fist. He was torn between going after her and letting her cool off on her own. If he went after her, it would soften his stance. Even as much as he cringed at the words that had come out of his mouth, he also knew this was for the best. She'd be mad. Her ego would be bruised, but she'd get over it in a day or two and then they could get back to the type of relationship they'd shared for the last several years. One that didn't involve him losing himself between her thighs.

He watched her retreating back as she walked stiffly into the distance. With a sigh, he started the engine and rammed the truck into gear.

Jasmine heard him roar off and rolled her shoulder in a dismissive gesture. She shouldn't be so pissed. But she wasn't going to sit there and take his posturing either.

Any woman, indeed.

Walking calmed her, some, even though the midday sun shone hot on her shoulders. She took her camera out and snapped several shots on her long trek back to the house.

Try as she might, she couldn't rid herself of Seth's words. Logically she knew she shouldn't let them get under her skin, but there wasn't much logic in emotion.

She trudged on, wiping at the sweat on her brow. She'd missed lunch, and dinner wasn't shaping up to be a very fun experience. She'd have to face Seth and Zane, both of whom were going to be uncomfortable around her for vastly different reasons.

So far she was making a mess of her intention to make them see that she was theirs. Always had been. It had all seemed so simple thousands of miles away in a foreign city. Go home, make them both love her as she loved them, convince them that a relationship between the three of them was possible.

What the living hell had she been thinking? How was she supposed to drop that kind of bomb on them and how would they react?

"You don't tell them anything," she muttered. "You show them. It's up to you to show them it could work."

She sighed and rubbed absently at her aching temples. No, dinner wasn't something she really wanted to experience tonight. Carmen was a stickler for family gatherings. If you were home, you were present and accounted for in the dining room. No excuses.

Which only left one possibility. Not being home.

The idea of going into town for the evening cheered her up considerably. She hadn't yet ventured into Barley. Tucker's bar had always been a source of fun, even if Seth and Zane had hauled her out of it on more than one occasion. At least now she was of legal age.

She grinned. A little hell-raising did sound like an awful lot of fun. And if she dressed a little sexy and managed to capture the attention of a few local boys, then all the better. Her ego could use a little rebuilding after Seth's putdown anyway.

She took her sweet time walking back to the ranch. It was late afternoon when she puttered up to the house, her shirt soaked with sweat and her hair clinging like limp noodles to her head.

When she walked through the patio door and into the kitchen, Carmen turned around and gasped. She immediately started rattling off a stream of Spanish, almost too fast for Jasmine to understand.

She smiled and held her hands up. "I'm fine, *mamacita*. English please. My head hurts too bad to keep up."

"That boy," Carmen sputtered. "Leaving my *niña* out God knows where. What was he thinking?" She threw her hands up in the air in exasperation. "I ask him when he comes in. 'Where is Jasmine?' He mumbles something about you walking back. Walking back! In this heat. Why did you not ride back with him, *niña*?"

"He made me angry," Jasmine replied. "And no, I don't want to talk about it. What I want is a cold shower and fresh clothes. Then I'm going into town for the evening, so don't hold supper for me."

Carmen opened her mouth to protest but Jasmine dropped a quick kiss on her cheek and headed for the stairs.

Seth was who knew where, and Zane's truck hadn't been here when she'd walked up. She didn't exactly have permission to use Seth's truck, but he had said in the past that she could use it when she needed it. If that was a year ago, oh well. She was annoyed enough with him not to care.

Chapter Eight

It took her half of the drive into town to get used to driving Seth's big-ass truck. She had to lean forward in the seat so she could see over the hood. But she made it to the bar just as dusk fell, and she couldn't wait to get inside and see who all was there.

She climbed out of the truck and ran her hands over her form-fitting jeans. Then she reached back into the cab and snagged her straw cowboy hat. She shoved it onto her head and glanced down to check her appearance.

Her cropped T-shirt hung just below her breasts, baring her belly ring and midriff. Her jeans rode low on her hips and clung to every curve on their way down. She smiled. She looked hot, damn it.

Any woman, my ass.

She walked into the bar and peered around the interior. Not much had changed. It was still smoky as hell, and the click clack of balls colliding on the pool table echoed from the back of the room.

A hard arm snaked around her waist and hauled her up against an equally hard chest.

"Jasmine, darlin', what the hell are you doing here?"

"J.T.!"

She turned her face up to smile at him. He dropped a kiss on her forehead then gestured to a nearby table. "Come have a seat with me."

She sighed and rolled her eyes. "Don't you mean come where you can keep an eye on me?"

He grinned and ushered her over to the table. "My days of tossing your ass out of the bar are over. You're legal now."

"Not worried I'll cause trouble?" she asked mischievously.

He winked as he sat down and held up two fingers at the passing waitress. "You and trouble are a given. It's only a matter of how much and when."

She shook her head and sat down across from him. "I wasn't that bad."

His green eyes twinkled at her. "Yes, you were. Kept me on my toes. Truth was, I looked forward to every weekend. I always wondered what scheme you'd concoct next."

She rolled her eyes. "It got boring out at the ranch. Seth and Zane were having all the fun."

"And now?" J.T. asked.

"Now, I left their sorry asses at home," she grumbled.

"In that case, try not to have too much to drink. I don't want to worry about you driving yourself home, and I damned sure don't want to have to lock you up for a DUI."

She chuckled at the concern in his voice. "Don't worry, J.T. If I have too much to drink, I'll crawl over to the hotel and stay over."

"Or you could just call Seth or Zane to come get you," he said pointedly.

"I'd prefer not."

J.T.'s brow creased. They were interrupted as the waitress plunked down two cold bottles of beer in front of them. Jasmine gripped her beer and took a sip as she surveyed the rest of the room.

"What's going on with you and those boys?" J.T. asked. "Not like you to want to avoid them when you've spent the last six years velcroed to them."

Jasmine winced. "Am I that obvious?"

"Not sure what you're getting on about, sweetheart. I just wondered if they'd done something to piss you off, and then I marveled at the idea of them being able to do something to make you angry." He chuckled and shook his head.

She raised the bottle to her lips again and took a long drink. "I'm just here to have a good time. No other reason."

He nodded and shrugged his shoulders. "Nothing wrong with that."

She raised her hand as the waitress walked by again. When she stopped, Jasmine leaned forward so the woman could hear. "Two shots of tequila please."

As she sat back, J.T. frowned disapprovingly.

"Now, J.T.," she drawled. "I said I'd crash at the hotel if I got too intoxicated. Besides, I'm driving Seth's truck, and I have no desire to find out what he'd do if I wrapped it around a telephone pole."

"Oh, shit."

"What?"

"Does Seth know you're driving his truck?"

"Well, he does now," she said with a grin.

J.T. chuckled. "It's going to be fun as hell to have you around again. I only wish I was there to see Seth shit a brick when he realizes you took off in his truck."

"What's the deal with his truck?"

"He loves that truck," J.T. said.

She shrugged. "I didn't see anything special about it."

J.T. snorted. "You wouldn't. It's a guy thing. He bought it six months ago. Custom paint job, big tires, roll bar with lights—you know, guy stuff."

She rolled her eyes. "A truck is a truck is a truck."

"I'll pretend I didn't hear that."

The waitress swung by and delivered Jasmine's shots. Jasmine gripped one of the small shot glasses in her hand and raised it toward J.T. "To Barley, Texas and being back home."

"I'll drink to that," J.T. said, raising his beer.

&

"What do you mean she went into town?" Seth demanded. "How the hell did she get there?"

Carmen frowned at his tone and tsked under her breath. "She drove. How else would she get into town unless you wanted her to walk like you made her do this afternoon?"

Seth sighed. "I didn't make her walk, Carmen. You know once Jasmine's made up her mind about something, there's little you can do to change it." And then another thought occurred to him, about the same time he realized that Zane wasn't home and hadn't been home all day. Which meant there was only one way Jasmine could have driven into town. He groaned even as he headed to the garage to see what he already suspected.

He stood in the doorway, bracing his hand on the frame as he stared at the empty space where his truck was usually parked. If she so much as put a scratch on it...

She'd be lucky if she didn't put herself in a ditch somewhere. She hadn't driven in the year she'd been in Paris, and before that, she'd always tooled around in Zane's smaller truck, not that she'd driven a lot even then. She'd always been content to tag along with him or Zane wherever they happened to be going.

But she wasn't a little girl anymore. Hell, she never had been. Even at sixteen she'd had more experience in her eyes than most women a dozen years older.

The memory of her mouth hot against his, her tongue bold and seeking, sent a bolt of awareness through his body. He closed his eyes, not wanting to relive the hurt in her eyes when he pushed her away.

"Seth, J.T. is on the phone for you," Carmen called from the kitchen.

He shut the door to the garage and walked back to where Carmen stood, phone in hand.

"Hey, man, what's up?" Seth asked as he put the phone to his ear.

"Not much. I've been down at the bar with your girl."

"Jasmine?" Annoyance inched a slow crawl over his shoulders. The idea of Jasmine hanging out with J.T. irritated the shit out of him. Nearly as much as the idea of her going out with Brad.

"I got called out. Domestic disturbance. On my way to it now. But when I left, she was on her way to throwing one hell of a drunk." J.T. hesitated for a moment. "It's not that I don't trust her. She said she'd get a hotel room if she wasn't able to drive home. I just worry about her. Something seemed to be bothering her. I thought you'd want to know."

Seth swore. "You did right. The last thing I want is for her to get hurt. I'm without wheels, but I'll call Zane. He's on his way home. I'll have him stop in and pick her up. In the meantime, I'll call Tucker and have him make sure Jasmine stays put until Zane gets there."

℘

The room was a little blurry. Okay, maybe a lot blurry. But she was having too much damn fun to worry about calling it a night.

Jasmine shook and shimmied, stomped her feet and clapped her hands in time with the country song the band was playing. More than one man was happy to dance with her. At least three skirted her periphery as she shook her head, hair flying.

One grasped her hand and spun her around where she collided with the chest of another. She smiled up as the second man put his hands on her shoulders and let them slide down her arms.

Yet another, too-tall, too-sexy cowboy pressed against her back, rotating his hips into her ass. Sweat beaded her forehead and her breath came heavier. How would it feel to be between Seth and Zane?

She closed her eyes and imagined for a moment that it was them who surrounded her body. She'd watched them one night. Saw them make love to the same woman. She'd been mesmerized by the sight and had been horribly jealous of the woman whose name she'd never even known. And then there was Mary Jo, town hairdresser. After seeing her between Seth and Zane, Jasmine had never been able to bring herself to go into Mary Jo's salon.

She'd wanted it to be her. Already confused by her feelings for both brothers, those interludes had given her a taste of what it would be like to have them both.

But it wasn't until she arrived in Paris and had met Cherisse that her secret fantasies had taken a serious flight into reality. Seeing her friend in a polyamorous relationship, a happy, loving situation, had given Jasmine hope that maybe she could love both men and that maybe they could love her in return.

When she'd told Cherisse about Seth and Zane, Cherisse had laughed and asked her why she was in Paris and not back in Texas.

As tempted as Jasmine had been to return, she also knew that the time away would do her—and them—good. She needed to spread her wings, prove her independence, and she also needed to return to them a woman. Not the needy, insecure girl they'd taken care of for so long.

And the truth was, as much as she'd missed home and Seth and Zane, Paris had been an amazing, wonderful experience. She wouldn't trade that year for anything.

She felt a hand slide up the bare skin of her abdomen and lodge just underneath her breast. Her gaze dropped to see one of her cowboys had gotten up close and personal. His hands rested possessively on her body, and he was shouldering away from the other two men who had circled around her to dance.

If she didn't nip this in the bud soon, he'd definitely get the wrong message.

She put her hand on his wrist, and his knuckles brushed the underside of her breast as she pried him away.

"Come on now, sugar," he murmured close to her ear. "Why don't you let me take you home and put you to bed? Preferably my home and my bed."

She smiled. "Sorry, cowboy. I'm just here for a good time."

"Oh, I could show you a good time," he purred.

Strong arms surrounded her, lifted her away from the cowboy in question and set her aside. Zane.

"She's off-limits," Zane said in a near growl.

She blinked because for some reason, Zane kept swimming out of her vision. And damn it, he looked too good to keep fading out like that.

Not hearing what the two were saying to each other, she snuggled up against Zane's side, and he dropped an arm around her in a protective gesture.

She rubbed her cheek against his shirt and inhaled his scent. He pulled her toward the door, and she wrapped her arm around his waist to steady herself.

The night air, warm and humid, hit her in the face as they stumbled outside. He walked her over to his truck and stopped as she leaned against the frame.

"Jaz, I don't know what to do about you," Zane said with a chuckle. "Seth is home having a kitten because you drove off in his truck, and J.T. is beside himself at the thought of you driving home drunk."

She frowned her irritation. "And what do you think?" she asked huffily.

He reached out and tweaked her nose. "I think you're damn cute when you're drunk."

She grinned and leaned closer to him. "You're pretty cute too." She wrapped her arms around his neck and pulled him closer to her.

"Jaz, honey," he whispered. "This isn't a good idea."

She silenced him with her lips. His arms tightened around her, bending her slightly backwards as her head tilted underneath his.

"I need you," she whispered back. "I ache. God, Zane, I hurt. I want you so much."

His mouth devoured hers hungrily, as if he'd waited a lifetime to kiss her like this. She whimpered against his lips, her body writhing, hot and needy against his.

He broke away. "Not here. Not like this, Jaz. Get in the truck."

Her entire body trembled as he opened the door and ushered her into the passenger seat. He closed the door once she was in then walked around the front to the driver's side.

Without a word, he started the engine and tore out of the parking lot like he was being chased by the devil.

Her hand fluttered to her lips, but they didn't ache nearly as much as other parts of her body. She twisted restlessly on the seat, stretching her body in an attempt to alleviate the tension.

Her belly ring flashed in the glow from the headlights. She could see Zane looking at it. Her belly. The ring. And then her breasts which just barely peeked out from underneath the cropped T-shirt.

"I hurt, Zane," she whispered.

He pulled onto a dirt road, fishtailing as he righted the truck. He drove a half mile before cutting the engine and dousing the lights. Then he reached for her, pulling her against him.

Her fingers twisted in his long hair as he cupped her face in his hands. Their lips met and both panted for breath as they moved hot against each other.

"Where do you hurt, baby?" he murmured against her lips.

"Here," she said, dragging one of his hands down her belly, lower to her pelvis and finally to rest at the juncture of her legs.

He groaned and rubbed his fingers over the denim covering her pussy.

"Touch me," she whispered.

His fingers fumbled with her snap. Then he worked the zipper down, parting the fly. He reached behind him to open his door. The "door ajar" pinging sounded abrasive in the air, and he yanked at the keys, letting them fall to the floorboard.

He got out and stood in the doorway. He gazed at her, eyes blazing in the dark.

"Lie back, sugar," he said in a strained voice. He pulled at her so that she was positioned with her legs dangling over his seat.

He peeled her jeans over her hips and down then yanked impatiently at her sandals so he could remove the pants.

He leaned forward, sliding his hands underneath her to cup her ass. He pulled until her knees pressed against his chest. She stared up at him, holding her breath in anticipation. She'd waited so long, wanting him, needing him, loving him so much.

He lowered his head to her belly and kissed her navel. The simple action sent shivers racing over her skin. His tongue lapped at her belly ring. He nibbled and toyed with it, finally sucking the delicate ring into his mouth.

"You like it?" she asked huskily.

"You know I do. You knew damn well it would make me crazy."

She smiled.

His fingers curled around the thin band of her panties and gently began tugging them down her hips. His mouth followed the progress, kissing the expanse of skin from her belly to her soft mound.

"Please," she whispered. "I need..."

"I'll give you what you need, sugar," he murmured. "Just this once."

She arched into him as his mouth found her clit. She bucked uncontrollably as shards of pleasure shot through her pelvis. Her stomach tightened and the muscles in her legs spasmed as his tongue worked over her delicate flesh.

Her hand tangled in his hair, pulling him closer, begging him not to stop.

He licked and nibbled in turn, his tongue swirling around her quivering bud. He moved his fingers to trace a lazy circle around her pussy entrance. She moaned, suddenly needing so much more.

"Shhh, baby."

He eased one finger inside just as he sucked her clit between his teeth.

"Zane!"

He chuckled. "You taste so sweet, Jaz. So sweet and fucking innocent. I'm going to hell for this, but damn, it's going to be an awesome ride."

"More," she whimpered. "Please. I need to come. I can't stand it anymore."

"Then come, baby. Come for me."

He thrust another finger inside, gently sliding the tip along the wall of her pussy. He sucked at her clit and moved his hand back and forth, creating the most delicious friction.

Her orgasm built and swelled, nothing like her self-induced pleasure escapades. God, this was the real thing, and it was so much more than she'd imagined.

As she writhed beneath him, he increased the tempo until finally, it felt as though she burst into one big ole explosion of ecstasy. She cried out, the sound sharp in the night.

He continued to coax her orgasm from her in long, sweet strokes of his tongue. She panted as the world spun around her. "Zane, Zane," she chanted.

Finally she went limp against the seat. He kissed her quivering flesh one last time before he pulled away. Gently, he pulled her underwear back up her legs, and then he reached for her jeans. He bent to retrieve her sandals and slid them over her feet.

Her limbs felt heavy and lethargic. Sleepy, satisfied contentment settled into her body. The warm buzz of alcohol mixed with the glow of her orgasm made movement damn near impossible.

"Scooch up, honey," Zane said in a low voice as he reached out a hand to help her up.

She struggled to sit up and move over to her seat as he climbed back in beside her. She blinked and stared at him as he started the engine.

"Zane?"

He looked over at her.

"You don't regret it do you?"

He paused for a long moment, guilt crowding his expression. "I shouldn't have done it, Jaz, but God help me I don't regret it."

Chapter Nine

As they drove up the winding driveway to the ranch house, Jasmine dreaded the thought of confronting Seth. She didn't really care if he was pissed about the truck. She wasn't ready to face him after the way he pushed her away, and especially not after Zane had just performed oral sex on her.

"I hope Seth didn't wait up," she said with a sigh.

Zane chuckled. "Tell you what. You pretend you're passed out, and I'll haul you upstairs to bed. You can face Seth in the morning."

She grinned as she remembered so many other nights where Zane had covered for her.

They pulled to a stop outside the garage, and Zane cut the engine.

"Let's be quick about this," Zane said as he hopped out. He walked around to her side and opened the door. He turned her legs around until she faced him sideways and then simply picked her up, placing his shoulder into her belly.

She swung over his back, her nose bumping against his back pocket. His arm curved over the back of her legs just below her ass, and when he started walking to the door, his hand slid possessively over her behind.

And sure enough, Seth met them as soon as Zane walked in. She guessed Zane must have held a finger to his lips and shushed Seth, because his question got aborted mid-sentence and he quieted.

Thankful that her face was hidden in Zane's back, she held her breath until Zane mounted the stairs and headed for her bedroom.

A few seconds later, he deposited her on the bed and stepped back. "Okay, sugar, here you are. Now get undressed and into bed. Sleep off this drunk. I'll make sure Carmen has a good hangover remedy for you in the morning."

He turned to go, but Jasmine called out to him in a voice just above a whisper. "Zane?"

He swiveled back around and gazed down at her.

"I knew exactly what I was doing," she said. "I'm not *that* drunk. I wanted you."

His throat worked up and down as he swallowed. His breath escaped him in a long sigh, whether frustration or unease she wasn't sure. Maybe a little of both.

Then he bent down and kissed her on the forehead. "Good night, Jaz. I'm going to go drive into town with Seth so we can get his truck."

She closed her eyes in disappointment at the significance of the tiny kiss. He was putting her solidly back on familiar ground.

When she opened them again, Zane was gone. She sighed and flopped back on the bed, arms spread. She tucked her hands behind her head and stared up at the ceiling.

They wanted her. She knew this. Knew that both Seth and Zane were attracted to her. Seth's words rang in her ears, and she wondered if maybe he was right. Maybe it was true for both of them. Maybe she could have been any woman.

That wasn't enough for her. She'd never be any woman. She'd be everything to them or nothing.

She sat up and struggled to get out of her clothes. Did she have any chance at making them love her in return? At making them see that she needed them both?

It won't be easy, chérie. The sort of committed relationship between the three of you that you propose is foreign to them. Aberrant. It will be up to you to show them how beautiful it can be.

Cherisse's caution floated around in Jasmine's mind. She'd discarded her friend's words at the time because she'd been too caught up in the idea of resolving her love for both men. Cherisse was right. It wouldn't be easy. But then what ever was?

She pulled herself up from the bed and trudged over to the window. Seeing Zane's truck gone, she deemed it safe to go crawl into the shower. She had a long night ahead of her if she was going to wait for Zane to return.

&

Jasmine watched from the window as the two trucks rolled up the drive nearly an hour later. She dropped her finger away from the curtain and quickly moved over to her bed. She crawled under the covers and waited.

Soon she heard the quiet footsteps in the hall and then heard them pause outside her door. She lowered her lashes until her eyes were half-lidded. To her surprise, Seth appeared around the doorway, his outline recognizable even in the darkened room. She shut her eyes as he moved closer.

She tried to breathe normally as he neared her bed. Then he stopped, and she was dying to know what he was doing. She opened her eyes just a crack, hoping that he couldn't see her in the dark.

He stood by her bed, staring down at her, an indecipherable expression on his face. Then he reached down to touch her hair. He ran his fingers over the strands and to her cheek. And like Zane, he bent and kissed her softly on the forehead.

"I'm sorry," he whispered.

He left the bed, his footsteps retreating across the room. She opened her eyes wider to see him walk out of her bedroom, closing the door behind him.

Her chest ached with the need to go after him. If only it was as easy as going to both of them, telling them she loved them and having them accept that her love encompassed them both.

Her fingers curled around the covers, and she let out a shaky breath, emotion knotting her throat. She turned over on her side and curled her knees to her chest. What if they never accepted it? What if they couldn't come to terms with the relationship as she saw it?

The idea sent panic swelling into her chest and stomach, twisting her insides until she clawed at her throat in an attempt to assuage the relentless ache.

She lay there for as long as she could stand it and then she got up. Silently, she cracked open her door and peered down the darkened hallway. Both Seth's and Zane's doors were closed. Her alcohol buzz long abated, she tip-toed down to Zane's door and slowly turned the knob.

When she entered, Zane looked up from his perch on the bed. He was sprawled on the bed, the covers pulled up to his waist. He held the TV remote in one hand and propped his body up on his other elbow.

"I thought you'd be long passed out," he said with a hint of discomfort in his voice. His hand clutched at the sheets and pulled them a little tighter to his waist.

She didn't speak. Didn't trust her voice not to betray her. Instead she walked over to the bed and crawled up onto the mattress, kneeling in front of him. With one hand, she reached out and tugged the sheet from his hand. It fell away, revealing an obvious erection.

"Were you thinking about me?" she asked softly, a hint of a smile twitching the corners of her mouth.

"Jaz, you need to go back to your room," he said in a near groan. He grabbed for the sheet, but she held fast. She was transfixed by the sight of his arousal.

Beautiful. Sleek. Yet completely male and rugged. She was staring shamelessly, and she didn't care. Dark hair surrounded the thick base, and his cock shot upward toward his firm belly.

"Were you thinking about me?" she repeated as she moved closer still.

"You know damn well I was," he said in a tight voice.

She ran her hand up his thigh, loving the hair-roughened surface of his skin. The muscles coiled and jumped beneath her fingers. Before she lost her nerve, she moved her other hand and curled her fingers around the base of his cock.

"Jaz..."

It was an intoxicating mixture of satiny softness with a core of steel. She slowly rolled her hand upward, marveling at how quickly it hardened even further in her palm.

"I want to taste you. Like you tasted me," she murmured as she leaned over his hips, her hair spilling over his groin.

"Jesus," he whispered with agonized strain.

Cautiously, she circled the head of his dick with her lips. His scent surrounded her, filled her as she inhaled. Tangy. Masculine. He tasted wild and warm. She worked her lips lower, sucking lightly as he rasped over her tongue.

His hips twitched and rocked upward. She moved her hand down, allowing her mouth to follow its progress. When the tip came to rest at the back of her throat, she eased back, squeezing with her hand and working back up in unison with her mouth.

Zane's hand tangled roughly in her hair. His fingers glanced over her scalp as if he was seeking purchase and finding none. She chanced a peek up his body when she reached the end of his cock with her mouth. His head was thrown back, eyes closed, an expression she could only describe as pain marring his face.

"Will you let me taste you?" she whispered. "Will you come in my mouth like I came in yours?"

He let out a string of curses. He sounded like a man who was losing the last vestige of control. In answer to her question, he surged upward, burying his cock in her mouth. His hand tightened in her hair as he held her in place.

His other hand found the hem of her nightshirt and he pulled upward. "Take it off," he muttered. "I want to see you."

She released his cock and rocked back on her heels. Her hands fumbled with his as they both yanked at her shirt. She pulled it over her head and tossed it to the floor.

Zane stared at her, his eyes glittering as his gaze fastened on her breasts. "Come here, baby. I want to taste them."

He pulled her forward, angling his mouth so that her nipple slid between his seeking lips. Pleasure rocketed through her abdomen, tightening her pussy until she squirmed.

"Like candy," he murmured. "So sweet and delicate." He nibbled at the rigid tip then coaxed her over so he could lap at the other.

She threaded her hand into his thick hair, holding him against her. His mouth, so hot and wet, sucked avidly at her breast and sent delicious shivers down her spine.

Then he released her, and he pushed impatiently at her shoulders, guiding her back down to his cock. "Finish it," he said huskily. "Make me come."

She lowered her head, once again grasping his cock, and guided it to her mouth. She closed her eyes and sucked him deep, allowing herself to revel in his taste and feel.

"That's it," he moaned. He stroked her hair, touched her face, feathered his fingers across her jaw as he pumped his hips up and down.

As she took him deep, his hands glided down her body to cup her breasts. He rolled her nipples between his fingers, alternating cupping the small globes with thumbing her stiff peaks.

"I'm going to come, baby. If you don't want me to come in your mouth, you need to move," he said in a strained voice.

She ignored him and sucked harder. She moved her hand from the base of his cock and wrapped her fingers around his sac. She loved the feel of the soft, puckered skin dotted with fine hairs. His balls tightened and rolled as she lightly squeezed.

His hand curled around the base of her neck and held her firmly in place as he buried himself one last time. Warm, salty fluid spurted into her mouth.

It felt thick and creamy as it spilled onto her tongue. She'd never experienced anything so erotic. She swallowed, opening her mouth so he could go deeper. She wanted him. All of him.

Finally he slumped back onto the bed, sliding from her mouth in the process. She stared up at him, and he stared back with lazy contentment. He reached out a thumb and wiped his fluid from her lips.

"Beautiful," he murmured. "So fucking wild and beautiful. I hope to God you never change."

She curled herself into his embrace, melting against his hard body. He wrapped his arms around her and rolled until they lay side by side.

"Don't make me go," she whispered. "Hold me just for tonight."

He leaned forward and kissed her softly on the lips. "We can't do this, Jaz."

She wanted to argue. Wanted to point out that there was no reason they couldn't other than his own personal hang-ups and the fact that Seth had probably already laid down the law. But she also knew she was going to have to be patient. Zane and Seth were worth it to her. It would take time, and she didn't want to push too hard too fast and ruin her chance at happiness.

So she nuzzled into his chest, closing her eyes as the warmth of his embrace bled into her body. "Then be angry at me tomorrow," she said. "But for tonight, I don't want to be alone."

Chapter Ten

Seth knew before he ever opened Zane's door that he shouldn't go looking for trouble. Still, he was compelled to see if Jasmine was once again in Zane's bed. It was early, not even light, and when he'd peeked in on Jasmine, he'd found her bed empty.

But he wasn't prepared for the sight that greeted him. Jasmine, naked, curled up next to Zane, who was also—naked.

His fingers clenched the knob and anger buzzed over him in a white hot flash. Zane's arm was thrown possessively over Jasmine, and his hand cupped one of her breasts. His cheek rested against her dark hair, and both were sound asleep.

He felt—betrayed.

Before he did something he knew he'd regret, he retreated, shutting the door behind him. He stood outside Zane's door for a long moment, trying to control the anger, and if he were honest, the jealousy that was fast taking over his rationality.

He stalked down the stairs and headed outside. His fists were still clenched, and he willed himself to calm down. He had no right to be pissed. He'd pushed Jasmine away. Been cruel to her. On purpose. She had every right to find comfort elsewhere.

But a large part of him was angry that she'd found it so soon. And with his brother.

What a goddamn mess.

He began unloading sacks of seed from the trailer, hoisting them to his shoulder and tossing them down in a row inside the shed. He worked mechanically, trying to numb his raw emotions.

He barely noticed sunrise, and only stopped to drag an arm over his damp brow when the sun had been up a good hour. His shoulders and arms ached from the continual lifting and tossing. But he only had a few sacks left.

"Hey bro, you should have waited on me," Zane said from behind him. "I told you I'd help you get those unloaded this morning."

Seth tensed and slowly rose to a standing position. He wiped his hands on his jeans and turned to face his brother.

"I figured you were otherwise occupied," he said in a clipped tone.

"What's that supposed to mean?" Zane asked. But he averted his eyes almost guiltily.

Which only made Seth angrier.

"What the hell are you doing fucking that little girl?"

Zane blinked, his expression shocked by Seth's outburst. Then his eyes narrowed and his lips thinned.

"She's not a little girl, Seth. You know it and I know it."

"I don't give a damn. You crossed the damn line. You know it and I know it," he said, tossing Zane's words back at him.

"What line is that exactly?" Zane demanded. "The one where you tell me how to act and feel? I've got news for you big brother. I don't need a goddamn babysitter, and I damn sure don't need you telling me who I can or can't fuck."

Seth saw red. No matter that he'd been just as crude. Hearing the words from Zane's mouth, the blatant disrespect enraged him. Even if it did make him a goddamn hypocrite.

Before he could think, before he could stop himself, he swung his fist, connecting with Zane's face. Zane's head snapped back, and his knees buckled for a split second before he recovered and lunged for Seth.

Well, fuck. It had been years since they'd gone to fist city, but as pissed off as Seth was, he could use a good barnyard brawl.

❧

Jasmine woke to sunshine streaming in through the window. Automatically she felt for Zane but once again was greeted by a cold, empty spot. She sighed and rolled over for a moment, hugging his pillow to her. One morning she'd like to actually wake in his arms.

Reluctantly, she pushed herself up and swung her legs over the side. Her head felt a little muggy, but at least it wasn't hurting. She searched around for her shirt and found it half hidden underneath the bed. She rose and pulled it on before padding to the door.

She cracked it and nervously looked out before slipping into the hallway. She hurried toward her bedroom and into the shower. Thirty minutes later, she collected her camera and headed downstairs to the small study that housed the computer.

Her hands shook as she sat down and fumbled with the USB cord that would enable her to download pictures from her camera to the computer.

She was scared to death to face Zane. And Seth. Seth had rejected her, and while Zane hadn't at first, he'd made it clear he considered what had happened a big mistake. She was making a first-class mess of her intentions, and worse, she was failing miserably in her quest.

After downloading her pictures, she checked her email, grateful once again that Seth had installed satellite internet for her.

She smiled as she read a quick note from Cherisse. The bubbly French girl always managed to cheer her up. She typed a quick response and sent it on its way.

As she scanned the rest of the emails in her inbox, her gaze focused on the subject header of one. *Wildscapes Magazine.* She clicked to open it and skimmed over the message.

Photos that she'd taken while in France, as well as older photos of the West Texas landscape, had been accepted for publication by *Wildscapes*. In addition they were very interested in other photos she might have and would like to know if she would consider a regular feature for their magazine—"Without Words", a photo column on a monthly basis.

She sat, stunned, then read back over the message again. Truthfully, she'd submitted them on a lark, in a moment of weak indecision before she'd determined that she would return to Sweetwater Ranch.

She eased back in her chair and stared for another long moment before sliding the cursor over the "X" to close the email program. She unplugged her camera and set it to the side then rolled her chair backwards to get up.

She should be excited. But how could she greet the news with enthusiasm when it would mean leaving Sweetwater? And the Morgan brothers.

Paris had been a catalyst for so many things. She'd gone there to find herself. She'd experimented, thrown herself into life away from the ranch, made new friends. But she'd been unable to escape the inevitable. She loved Seth and Zane. Would always love them. That wouldn't go away with time, distance or newfound maturity.

She trudged down the stairs, hungry and wanting the comfort of Carmen's company. But when she walked into the kitchen, she was greeted by a sniff and a reproving look.

Not what she needed today. Was everyone mad at her? She plopped down onto a barstool and propped her elbows on the counter.

"Good morning to you, too, *mamacita*."

Carmen stared balefully at her. "Hungry, *niña*? You're awfully late for breakfast. I should make you wait for lunch."

Jasmine sighed. "Why are you angry with me, *mamacita*?"

Carmen ignored her and bustled around the kitchen plating some of the leftovers from breakfast. She thrust the plate into the microwave and stood, hands on her hips as she waited for the time to lapse.

The door from the patio opened and shut and Jasmine swiveled on the stool to see who had come in. She gasped when she saw Zane standing there, rumpled, dirty, his mouth bleeding and his eye blackened.

Before she could open her mouth to ask him what the hell had happened, his lips tightened, and he strode out of the kitchen in the opposite direction.

She turned back to Carmen. "What on earth happened?"

Carmen huffed and plunked the plate down in front of Jasmine. "You are what happened, *niña*. You and these games you are playing with the boys."

Jasmine shook her head in confusion.

"They fight," Carmen said in exasperation. "I go outside and the two of them are rolling around in the dirt trying to kill one another. It's no way for brothers to behave."

Jasmine felt sick. She shoved the plate away, unable to stomach the thought of eating. She buried her face in her hands. "Oh, God, I never meant for this to happen."

Jasmine heard the ruffle of Carmen's skirts, and then she was enfolded in Carmen's arms. Carmen coaxed her hands from her face and cupped her chin in her hand.

"You're playing with fire. You know this, eh *niña*?"

"I love them, *mamacita*. What would you have me do?"

Carmen's face softened and she hugged Jasmine to her. "I know you do. But these boys. They're stubborn. They won't be easy to win over."

Jasmine nodded as Carmen moved back toward the stove to stir the chili she was making.

"What are your plans, *niña*? Now that you are home from Paris. What will you do now?"

The earlier email floated through Jasmine's memory. She leaned forward, resting her chin on her upturned palm. "I don't want to do anything. Is it so terrible that I don't want my life to take me away from here? This is my life. It's where I belong."

Carmen walked over to stand close to her once more. "Listen to me, *niña*. You can't put all your eggs in one basket. Because if that basket falls, all the eggs break and you have no more. You can't put your life on hold waiting on something that may never happen."

Jasmine winced even as she knew Carmen spoke the truth. She did have to plan for a future that may not include Seth or Zane.

"Oh, Carmen, what am I going to do?"

She let all the pent-up despair spill over. Carmen hugged her close and stroked her hair soothingly. "You're young, *niña*. Young and beautiful. You have your entire life ahead of you."

"But I don't want a life without them," Jasmine said quietly. "I realize how dramatic it may sound. You think I'm young. I don't know my mind. That this is all some crush that will fade as soon as the next hunky guy comes along."

She broke off but Carmen remained silent, waiting patiently for her to have her say.

"I left here, *mamacita*. I left here with the intention of not coming back. I didn't think I could ever have what I wanted, that there wasn't a way for me to win their love. I wanted to exert my independence. Make them see me not as someone they were stuck taking care of, but as a strong, independent woman capable of making it on her own.

"But my time in Paris only made things clearer to me. I was being a coward by running away. I never once stayed and fought for them. How can I expect them to see if I wasn't able to show them? And so here I am, wanting so much but no idea of how to make this work."

Carmen sighed. She drew away and framed Jasmine's face in her hands. "Sometimes, *niña*...sometimes we don't get what we want. You have to prepare yourself for the possibility that you may never get what it is you most want. And more than that, you have to figure out what you're willing to risk in your attempt to gain your heart's desire. Because if you fail in this, your relationship as it is now with Seth and Zane can never be the same."

"All or nothing," Jasmine said simply. "I understand what you're saying, *mamacita*. But I've already thought about that. I know if this doesn't work out, things can never be the same. It's a risk I'm willing to take."

"Then I will pray very hard for you to succeed, *mi niña*. I love you dearly, and I want what any mother wants for her daughter. I want you to be happy."

Jasmine hugged Carmen tightly. "I love you," she said, her voice muffled by Carmen's shoulder. "I never want to do anything to disappoint you."

Carmen patted her back and pulled away to look her in the eye. "I am very proud of you, Jasmine. You know your mind. I've never doubted that for a moment. Your convictions are strong."

"Let's hope they're strong enough," Jasmine said. "I have a feeling they're going to be sorely tested."

∞

Jasmine spent the rest of the day sequestered in the study with her computer. She answered the email from *Wildscapes* and made arrangements for them to fax a contract for her to sign. But she declined the offer for a regular column.

It may have been stupid, but she simply would not entertain that her future was anywhere but here at the ranch. And if worse came to worst and she was forced to consider a path that would take her away from Seth and Zane, she'd consider her options then.

At one point, she fell asleep at the desk, her head pillowed on her arms. She awoke when Carmen gently shook her.

"Go on up to bed, *niña*. The boys have gone to their rooms for the night."

Jasmine rubbed her eyes and glanced at the clock. It was nearly midnight. "Goodnight, *mamacita*. I love you."

"I love you too," she said, kissing Jasmine on both cheeks before she left the study.

Jasmine stood and stretched then shuffled out of the room. When she reached the top of the stairs, she stared down the hall at both closed doors. She walked down to Zane's room and quietly tried the knob, only to find it locked.

Hurt swelled and knotted in her throat. He was shutting her out.

The ache in her chest only grew as she trudged to her room. She closed the door behind her as she slipped in, and she leaned heavily against it.

She slid down the smooth wood until she crouched on the floor, and she drew her knees to her chest, hugging them tightly. What would she do? How could she force Seth to see her, to really see her?

Her plan had seemed so simple. But things in theory always did. It was easy to dream of how it would be, and that all she had to do was return, show them that she loved them and everything would fall into place.

Apparently she was a naïve idiot. So much for growing up. Maybe they were right. Maybe she was too young for them. Maybe she was just a silly little girl playing at being a woman.

But damn it, her love for them was real. It wasn't some misplaced adolescent crush. She'd had those. She knew the difference.

And she'd never been flighty. She'd made up her mind very early on that she wanted Seth and Zane. Even when the opportunity came up for intimate relationships with other men, she'd held back, reserved that part of herself for Seth and Zane. Her body was too important, as was her self-respect.

She'd always known she would only ever give such an important part of herself to someone she really loved. It didn't make her old fashioned or a martyr. It made her smart and damn choosy.

At the rate she was progressing with Seth and Zane, she might well die a virgin.

She heaved an aggravated sigh. It was time to quit feeling sorry for herself. She'd suffered a setback, but it wasn't the end of the world. She could either wimp out or she could move on and form a new plan of attack.

Chapter Eleven

The next few days tested her fortitude. Seth and Zane both avoided her, and when Seth was forced into contact with her, he was stiffly polite.

If he'd ever acted that way before, Jasmine would have immediately called him on it, but she wasn't ready to provoke him. Yet. She needed to think of a way around his iron-clad wall.

Zane, on the other hand, just avoided her. Once she'd nearly bumped into him on her way out of the kitchen, and his expression had become shuttered. He'd looked away before finally retreating.

She'd made a mistake thinking it would be easier to win Zane over first. She'd used their history of closeness as a point in her favor, but all she'd done was make things difficult between him and Seth. In hindsight, it should have been obvious that she was going to have to work on Seth first.

And so, with that in mind, she concocted a plan. While risky and a bit outlandish, it made her positively gleeful when she anticipated the outcome. It was just diabolical enough to work.

For the first time since the morning of Seth and Zane's fight, she felt upbeat and positive. She dressed in a pair of cutoff shorts and a form-fitting tank top that showed off the diamond teardrop belly ring.

Seth would probably have a coronary if she took off in his truck again, and she wanted him in the best possible mood for when she enacted her grand scheme. So she sucked up her courage and went in search of Zane.

She found him out working on a section of fence near the storage sheds. She stopped at a distance, unable to keep from admiring his bulging muscles and his sweat-slicked body. He paused for a moment and shoved his hair back from his face. It hung down on his shoulders, limp and slightly curly from the humidity.

When he looked up and saw her, she started forward, not wanting to give him the opportunity to escape.

"Zane?" she called softly.

He shifted a little uncomfortably, and then as if realizing there wasn't an escape route, he faced her again.

"Can I borrow your truck to run into town? I won't be gone long, I promise."

He looked a little relieved, and she wondered crossly if it was because she was leaving.

"Yeah, sure," he said as he dug into his pocket for the keys. He drew them out and tossed them into the air.

She caught them against her chest. "Thanks."

"We really need to get you your own set of wheels," he said. "Something you'd be comfortable driving."

She smiled and gave him a little wave. "I'm perfectly okay with driving yours. I'll see you later."

She walked away, not looking back, though she wanted nothing more than to go to him. She wanted to kiss him. Wanted him to take her in his arms. Take her back to the house and to his bed. She sighed. Hopefully soon. Patience had never been one of her finer virtues.

℧

Once she saw J.T.'s truck outside the police station, she parked beside him and walked inside. The cool air was welcome after only a few moments in the sweltering heat. Summer had come early and with a vengeance.

She smiled at the secretary and motioned toward J.T.'s office. "Is he busy?"

Sandra, who'd been the Barley police department's secretary since before most of its employees were born, smiled and waved her on by.

Jasmine stuck her head inside J.T.'s door and said, "Knock, knock."

J.T. looked up in surprise and swung his feet off his desk. They landed with a thump as he righted himself. "Hey girl, what are you doing here?"

"You got a minute?" she asked a little nervously as she walked further inside. "I have a small favor to ask."

He checked his watch. "I've got more than a minute. You want to grab lunch? I'm starving."

She grinned. "Sounds good. I left the ranch before Carmen had lunch finished."

They went two doors down to a small café that only stayed open from eleven to two every day for lunch. After they'd been seated and their orders taken, J.T. took a long drink of his tea and focused his attention on Jasmine.

"Now what can I do for you, sweetness?"

Heat crept into her cheeks, and she felt some of her courage desert her. She took a drink of her ice water, praying it would calm her embarrassment a little.

She cleared her throat as J.T. continued to look inquisitively at her. "I wondered if...uhm..." She leaned forward so that no one would overhear and whispered, "I wondered if you had an extra set of handcuffs I could borrow."

His eyes widened in surprise. His lips parted, and then he closed them again. "I know I'm probably going to regret asking this, but why on earth do you need handcuffs?"

"Do I have to say?" she asked.

J.T. chuckled. "Oh boy. Tell me it's legal at least."

She pretended to consider for a moment. "Well, you know Texas has some pretty funky sex toy laws..."

He hooted with laughter and shook his head. "You're serious. You want handcuffs?"

She sighed and sat back in her chair. "I'm desperate, okay? I need a way to make someone stay in one spot long enough for me to do a little convincing."

"Damn. What a lucky son of a bitch. Darlin' if you ever want to convince me, I can guaran-damn-tee that you won't need handcuffs. Unless you really, really want them," he added with a wicked grin.

They were interrupted when the waitress put their plates down in front of them. After she left, Jasmine chewed on a fry and glanced over at J.T. "So can I have them?"

J.T. gave her a thoughtful look. "Sure, I have a pair. Just don't be telling your unwilling partner that you got them from me. Oh, and make damn sure you don't lose the key."

She chuckled. "Thanks, J.T. You're a prince."

༓

Jasmine returned to Sweetwater a bit more cheerful than she'd left. J.T. always lifted her spirits. They went way back. Or at least the few years he'd spent hauling her out of Tucker's bar when she managed to sneak in. He'd spent almost as much time looking out for her as Seth and Zane.

She tossed Zane's keys on the kitchen table as she walked through, and she cocked her ear, listening for any sounds within the house. She could hear Carmen's television from her room, but the house was otherwise quiet.

Seth and Zane had either gone out or they were locked in their rooms avoiding her. Well, that was fine because Seth's time was limited. One way or another, things were going to come to a head. Just as soon as she got the chance to use those handcuffs.

Chapter Twelve

Zane leaned against the back porch railing and stared up at the broad expanse of stars twinkling against an inky black sky. He took a swig of his beer and set the bottle down on the wooden rail. Night sounds echoed across the terrain. In the distance a coyote howled, and closer, an owl hooted, followed by another a little further away.

As he took another sip of his beer, the bottle rubbed across the split in his lip, and he grimaced.

This was one time he was actually grateful to Seth for trying to kick his ass. Though Seth had certainly not escaped unscathed. Zane grinned then winced as he once again irritated his sore lip.

They both looked like shit, and while Zane couldn't speak for Seth, Zane *felt* like shit. They'd had plenty of squabbles over the years. What brothers hadn't? But never over a woman. Not one they both obviously had feelings for.

But the episode had forced Zane to examine a simple truth he'd been avoiding ever since Jaz had returned home. His feelings for her had changed. But the confrontation had also made him consider that for the first time, he and Seth were going to be at major odds. Zane didn't see a way around it. He wasn't willing to push Jaz away just because Seth thought it was the right thing to do.

He honestly had no idea how things would work out. Triangles were things of soap operas. Oddly enough, the idea that Jaz might have feelings for Seth didn't bother him as much as he might have thought. In a twisted way, he imagined she probably did have feelings for them both. That he could deal with. The idea of Jaz not being part of his life in some way? *That* bothered him.

He downed the last of his beer and headed back inside. It was dark in the kitchen. Carmen had long since retired. She wasn't exactly thrilled with him and Seth since their fight, and she hadn't gone out of her way to be accommodating.

As he walked through the living room, he saw Jaz asleep on the couch, the television still on. He quietly walked over and took the remote from her hand. He pointed it back at the TV and turned it off.

He laid the remote down on the end table by the lamp and stood there looking down at her. She was curled into a tight ball, one fist tucked under her chin. Her long dark hair spilled over her shoulders, satiny and fine. He reached down to touch her cheek, unable to resist the temptation.

She sighed and nuzzled closer to his hand. For a moment, he thought she'd awakened, and he tensed, not prepared to explain why he was standing over her, but she snuggled deeper into the couch and resumed her even breathing.

He relaxed in relief then reached for the afghan folded at the end of the couch. He pulled the blanket over her and gently arranged it so she was covered. Then he walked away.

ജ

It rained all morning and well into the afternoon. Jasmine stayed away from areas where she was likely to run into Seth and Zane. It wasn't that she dreaded the confrontation. But the next time she got close to either of them, it certainly wasn't going to be because she wanted a long, drawn-out conversation.

She had no idea what to say to either of them yet anyway. Her feelings were complex. There was no simple way to articulate them. She was having a difficult enough time sorting through them herself without having to explain them to someone else.

Her preference was to show them her love. Make them see it, feel it. She'd never taken sex lightly, not since that night in Houston when she'd been forced to barter her body. In her mind, she was giving them a gift she'd never shared with anyone else. Her soul.

She locked herself in the study and piddled on the computer for most of the afternoon. Her latest project was creating a website for Sweetwater Ranch. Once finished, complete with all the guided hunt information and pricing, she was going to talk to Seth and Zane about launching it and advertising on a few online sites.

A knock sounded at the door, and Jasmine looked up from her computer to see Carmen bustle through with a tray in hand.

"I trust this lunacy will come to an end soon?" Carmen said in exasperation. "It's ridiculous the three of you avoiding each other like this. It's no way for a family to behave."

"You're right, *mamacita*. It's not," Jasmine quietly agreed. "But I have to warn you it might get worse before it gets better. If it ever does."

Carmen set the tray down on Jasmine's desk with a thump. "You sound as though you've already given up, *niña*. What happened to your 'take on the world' attitude? Besides, if you ask me, it can't get much worse than it is now."

It could, but Jasmine didn't like to dwell on that possibility. Seth could always ask her to leave, or worse, he could remain so indifferent, so sealed off from her, that she would choose to leave. This time for good.

Carmen sighed. "Eat, *niña*. You don't need to miss any meals. You never would eat when you were upset."

"Thank you," Jasmine said with a small smile.

Carmen walked out, and Jasmine picked at her food with little enthusiasm. Butterflies danced in her stomach which made putting anything on top of them impossible.

Tonight was the night. Seth and Zane had been forced inside all day by the rain, and she knew they'd both go to bed early. She opened the desk drawer and pulled out the pair of handcuffs J.T. had given her. Next she picked up the thin piece of satin ribbon she'd secured the key to. She let it dangle from her fingertips and swing like a pendulum.

She turned to look out the window as she heard the rain resume. Water sluiced down the glass panes in rivulets, and in the distance, thunder rumbled.

She glanced back at the time on the computer. An hour. She'd wait an hour before venturing out. Then she'd head up to Seth's bedroom where she planned to take matters into her own hands.

Seth had never really considered himself a coward before now, but after days of avoiding the inevitable confrontation with Jasmine, he knew he was a first-class pansy.

He had no idea what to say to her, and he knew that whenever they did finally come face-to-face, their relationship would undergo a radical transformation. And probably not for the better.

Part of him longed for the simpler days when she was much younger and very off-limits. It had been a beautiful thing to behold to watch her shed the frightened, insecure mantle and blossom into a confident, beautiful young woman. But with that awareness, that growth, came the knowledge they could never go back to the innocent relationship they'd shared.

He sighed as he sank down onto his bed. He was damned tired, and he hadn't even done anything today beyond watch it rain. His family was in tatters. Zane was pissed and brooding. Jasmine was avoiding them both. Carmen was walking around in a perpetual huff, and the only food she'd dished up was what could be warmed in a microwave.

It was time for him to stop putting off the inevitable. He needed to face Jasmine. Apologize for being an ass but make it clear he'd stepped over the line and it wouldn't be happening again. Then he needed to make things right with Zane.

If Zane and Jasmine... He swallowed and shook his head. He hadn't even been able to complete the thought. If his brother had feelings for Jasmine, and if she returned them, then did he have any right to step between them? Especially if he had no intention of ever acting on his own attraction?

He rubbed his hands over his face in irritation. What a goddamn drama. Why couldn't things just go back to the way they were?

He yanked the covers back and then stood to undress. He was tired, moody and quite frankly, he couldn't wait for another day to begin. Maybe then he could get rid of the angst knotting his damn belly.

Chapter Thirteen

She stood beside the bed, watching him sleep. For several long moments, she didn't move. She barely breathed. She merely watched the smooth rise and fall of Seth's chest. The sheets were in a bunch at his waist, and she could just see the waistband of his boxers resting below his navel. One arm rested across his taut belly while the other lay on the pillow next to his head.

It was all Jasmine could do not to reach out and touch him. To trace the lines of his body, curving around the firm muscles and ridges. She wanted to bathe the room in light so she could see better, but that would have to wait.

Carefully, she lifted the handcuffs and moved closer to the bed. No sound betrayed her as she leaned over to secure one cuff around one of the slats of the headboard. She held her breath as she snapped it in place, relieved that there was barely a discernable click.

Her heart began racing as she inched toward his wrist. She would have to be fast. No stealth about this part. Reach and snap before he could react. Then back the hell away and get the lights. She was just grateful he didn't sleep with his gun close by. All she needed was to be mistaken for an intruder.

She took a deep breath, held it, grabbed his wrist with one hand and snapped the handcuff around it with the other. He jerked in surprise and she stumbled backward, her hand seeking the light switch.

"What the fuck?" Seth exploded just as her hand collided with the wall. She swiped and hit the light switch.

He threw his free arm over his eyes and tried to sit up, but his manacled wrist made it awkward. He threw his arm down and locked onto Jasmine with his furious gaze.

He glanced at his cuffed wrist. Then back at Jasmine. She stood, knees shaking with a combination of adrenaline and fear.

"Jasmine, what the fuck kind of stunt are you pulling?" he demanded. "Get me the hell out of these handcuffs. Now."

She stiffened her spine, put her chin up and stepped forward, her gaze never wavering from his. She didn't respond. The time for words wasn't now. He was probably too pissed to listen anyway.

She let her fingers flutter down to the snap of her jeans. She fumbled for a second before releasing the fly. The sound of her zipper easing downward made him frown even harder.

"Jasmine, I don't know what you're trying to pull, but don't...goddamn it, Jasmine, put your pants back on."

She smiled and stepped out of the confining denim. She'd worn lacy panties, barely a scrap. But they were feminine and sexy. Slowly and with great care, she slid her hands up her hips until her fingers brushed the bottom of her shirt.

She curled her hands underneath the hem and began tugging upward. Seth swore again. "Jasmine, stop it. You don't want to do this."

She ignored him and pulled the shirt over her head, leaving her in just her bra and underwear. She reached into the vee of her bra and pulled the key to the handcuffs free. She let it fall to her skin where it dangled from the satin ribbon she wore around her neck.

One step. Then another. Her knees bumped the edge of the bed, and she met Seth's heated gaze once more. She fingered the key, pulling it away from her chest so he could clearly see it.

"This is the key to the handcuffs," she said softly. "You get it when you get close enough to touch it. If you still want out by then."

She let the taunt land with just the right amount of challenge. His eyes narrowed, but they never left her body.

"Let me out," he gritted through his teeth. "If this is your attempt at manipulation—"

She reached behind her to tug at the hook on her bra. "Manipulation?" She shrugged. "I suppose, if that's the way you want to view it. I prefer to think of it as taking the initiative."

The bra straps slid from her shoulders, and she momentarily held the cups in place before finally allowing them to fall from her body.

He looked as though he was prepared to launch into another demand, so she inserted her fingers under the filmy band of her panties and began to slide her underwear down her legs.

She heard his intake of breath at the same moment he looked away. His jaw was set, so firmly clenched she could see the strain in his face.

"Seth." He didn't turn toward her. "Look at me," she said.

With seeming reluctance, he turned his head to face her once more.

"See me," she whispered.

His eyes tracked her movement as she knelt on the bed. She leaned toward him, her hair falling over her shoulders. She reached for the sheet, tugging until it came away from his body.

The bed shook as he yanked at his wrist. "Goddamn it, Jasmine, this has gone far enough." His voice was furious and laced with an edgy, needy coarseness that excited her.

"What will you do, Seth?" she asked mildly. "Call for help? Do you think Zane will come to your rescue? Or maybe Carmen?"

She dropped the sheet and crawled closer to his hips, careful to stay just out of arm's reach. His erection was straining against his boxers, and if he shifted so much as a centimeter, his cock would slide right through the slit in the front.

A little nudge ought to do it.

She pulled at the cotton material and watched in fascination as his cock broke free of constraint and jutted upward. He grabbed at his shorts with his free hand, trying to arrange them back.

She stopped him with her hand. It was chancy, getting close enough that he could grab her. But she knew he wouldn't hurt her. He might secretly devise a scheme to kill her, but it would remain fantasy. Just like hers was to lick every single inch of his skin.

When she wrapped her fingers around his hard cock, he groaned. In fascination, she worked her hand up and down, enjoying the silken smoothness of his skin. So soft. Incongruous with the thread of steel she could feel just beneath that satiny layer.

His hand fell away, hitting the bed at his side. She inched closer, inserting her knee between his thighs. At first he tensed as though he'd lock her out, but as she became more insistent, he relaxed.

Soon she crawled between his legs, and she chanced a look up at him. He watched her through half-lidded eyes. His gaze still burned with anger, but it also simmered with lust. Need.

"Do you know what I'm going to do?" she whispered. She continued working up and down in a slow motion, her fist gripping his cock in a tight sheath. "I'm going to make you so crazy, you'll beg me for mercy."

"Never," he gritted out.

She smiled then. The smile of a woman confident in her power of seduction. He'd thrown down the gauntlet and they both knew it.

Her hand fell away from his cock, and she dug her fingers into the waistband of his shorts. She pulled, but he wasn't cooperating. She couldn't budge his big body.

She sat back and smirked. "Surely you don't think something as insignificant as that will deter me?"

He looked suspiciously at her as she got up from the bed. She walked naked to the door and opened it. She glanced back at him, nearly laughing at his look of astonishment. "Oh, I'll be back," she said.

"Damn it, Jasmine, you can't go parading around butt-ass naked."

She arched a brow. "Who's going to see me?" She turned and left him swearing from the bed.

She darted down to her room to get the pair of scissors she should have thought to bring in the first place. When she returned a moment later, Seth was hard at work trying to break the headboard.

He stopped when he saw her, and he looked a little worried as he stared at the scissors in her hand.

She continued on and resumed her spot on the bed. She held the scissors up then neatly slid them underneath the leg of his shorts. "I'd be very still if I were you," she murmured.

"When did you get so goddamn evil?" he demanded.

"When did you get so goddamn stubborn?"

She sliced through his shorts, and after a few more strategic cuts, the material fell away to bare him completely. He shifted his hips as if trying to escape or roll over, but she straddled his legs. She loved the hair-roughened scratch of his skin over the tender insides of her thighs.

"Now to make you beg," she murmured.

She felt him stiffen. His muscles bunched and rolled underneath her. She splayed her hands over his hips, bent down and gently blew on his cock.

He shivered.

Growing bolder and more confident by the minute, she flicked out her tongue and licked the tip. His cock jumped, and she moved her hand from his hip to encircle the base.

"Jasmine, you have to stop. We can't do this. You have no idea what you're starting."

She slid the head past her lips and let her tongue dance around the edge. She smiled as he swore again. Slowly and with exacting precision, she inched lower, taking him further into her mouth. He was protesting far too much with no conviction.

He tasted rugged and hard, just like he looked. She squeezed her hand a little tighter, exerting firmer pressure as she worked her mouth up and down.

Then she sucked her way to the top and released his cock. "Do you want me to stop?" she asked huskily. "Really?"

"No goddamn you, I don't want you to stop."

"Tell me you want me."

His mouth closed in a firm line as he glared at her. She moved a little higher, leaning forward. Her hair brushed across his belly, and she released his dick. The tip bumped her in the stomach as she rose over him.

"Tell me, Seth," she said breathlessly.

His hand flew up and grabbed at the key hanging from the ribbon. He yanked and freed it. She glanced down in dismay as he palmed the key then jammed it into the lock of the cuffs.

Her hopes fell.

He jerked his arm free and flung the cuffs across the room. Then he rose up and yanked her to him. Her body fell against his hard chest at the same time their lips collided.

His hands tangled in her hair as he kissed her in breathless abandon. He rolled, taking her with him, tucking her underneath his body as her back met the mattress.

"I want you," he growled. "Happy? Now we'll see who begs."

Chapter Fourteen

Jasmine stared up at Seth, barely able to breathe for his body pressed tight to hers. His swollen cock nudged impatiently at the juncture of her legs. She wiggled and spread her thighs, wanting him closer. God, she wanted him inside her.

He leaned in and slanted his lips over hers. They fit so perfectly. He nibbled roughly at the corner of her mouth then licked at the seam until she opened to him.

She tasted him, feasted on him, each kiss, each touch making her want more, need more. All the waiting had been worth this one moment. Finally she had come home. To his arms. Where she belonged.

"I have to have you," he gasped into her mouth.

His knee forced her thighs wider apart, and he fit himself to her. She moaned and arched into him as the head of his cock probed her entrance. All the tiny nerve endings came alive and jumped as he slid forward.

He pushed forcefully into her, his impatience evident in his tense movements. She stiffened, surprised by the initial discomfort. Believing it would pass quickly, she wrapped her arms around him and held him closer.

He plunged deeper, and this time, she couldn't stop the small whimper that tore from her mouth. He stopped immediately, buried deep within her pussy.

He raised himself off her and looked her in the eye, an expression of stunned disbelief etched on his face. "Jesus Christ, Jasmine, you were a virgin?"

"It's all right," she said.

"No, it's not goddamn all right."

She lay there, his cock stretching her tissues painfully. There wasn't a part of her body that didn't feel him. It was a lot better when they were still in the foreplay stage.

Finally in Seth's bed, in his arms, and all she could do was think about how miserable she was. Tears pricked her eyelids and threatened to spill over the rims.

Seth swore softly and lowered his forehead to hers. He tenderly kissed away the tears that trickled down her cheeks. Then he slowly eased his cock out of her aching pussy. She flinched when he pulled free and rolled away.

He got up and strode to his dresser. Yanking out a pair of shorts, he pulled them on and looked back at her. "I'll be right back, don't move."

She watched as he disappeared from the bedroom then she closed her eyes as more tears spilled down her cheeks. It wasn't supposed to have hurt so damn much. In her mind, she'd figured he wouldn't even realize she was a virgin, and he probably wouldn't have if she hadn't made such a scene.

Seth returned a few seconds later, and she wouldn't look at him as he walked back over to the bed. She gasped in surprise when he put a cool washcloth between her legs and tenderly cleaned her flesh.

He reached out his fingers, slid them underneath her chin and forced her to look at him.

"Are you okay?" he asked quietly.

She swallowed and nodded.

"I'm sorry, Jasmine."

The anger in his voice gave her pause. She stared up at him, trying to figure out who he was angry with.

"I should have told you," she said in a low voice.

"Yes, you should have," he agreed. "But more than that, I never should have damn well touched you." He paused and looked away briefly before returning his gaze to her. "Damn it, Jasmine, I thought you had slept with Zane."

Her eyes widened. "He told you that?"

Seth frowned. "Of course not. Zane wouldn't talk about you like that."

"Then where would you get that idea?"

"I saw you. In bed with Zane. Both of you were naked and wrapped tight around each other. What was I supposed to think?"

Heat bloomed in Jasmine's cheeks. She wasn't supposed to feel guilty. In fact, she needed to be upfront about the fact that she loved both of the brothers. Otherwise how would she have a chance of making the relationship work?

Seth's jaw was drawn in an angry line. "What the hell were you trying to prove, Jasmine? What's gotten into you?"

Her mouth dropped open. "Why are you so angry, Seth? What does it look I was trying to do? I was trying to get you to see me as something more than the pathetic little girl you've been looking after. I wanted you to see me as a woman. As someone you might care for, damn it."

"It's obvious you're not a little girl anymore," he said through gritted teeth.

"Do I never have a chance at making you care for me, Seth?"

He looked at her in confusion. "What do you mean?"

"I love you. I've always loved you. I came back because I wanted the chance to make you love me."

Her announcement hung in the air as shocked silence followed. He didn't look happy with her declaration. If anything, he looked even more pissed.

She wished she could call back the words. He wasn't ready to hear them, and she hadn't been ready to say them. Not yet. She shrugged indifferently, trying to shield herself from the hurt crowding her chest. "We had sex, Seth. I don't see what the big deal is."

He stood, seething. He stared at her, a storm cloud gathering in his eyes. "No big deal, Jasmine? If it was no big deal then why did you save yourself all these years? I had no right to touch you. Not after..."

"Not after what?" Jasmine asked quietly.

Guilt and self-loathing shone in his expression. "I swore I'd never touch you after that night in Houston. Swore you'd never feel like you had to offer your body to me for payment or repayment. You offered yourself to me for sex when you were sixteen, something no girl should ever have to do. I refused then, but I still took you up on that offer. Just six years later. What kind of a man does that make me?"

He turned away, and she gasped in shocked anger. He started to walk out. Her words stopped him for a moment.

"If you can't tell the difference between the girl I was then, and the woman I am now... If you can't tell the difference between a girl offering herself to you out of desperation and a woman giving herself to you because she loves you, then there's not much I can say, is there?"

He stiffened, his back to her. His fingers curled into balls at his sides, and then he walked out of the bedroom, leaving her there to stare after him.

Chapter Fifteen

Jaz looked sad, a sight that didn't sit well with Zane at all. Her beautiful eyes were shadowed and reserved, not at all expressive and vibrant like they usually were.

He watched her eat breakfast and nod occasionally at what Carmen was chattering about. Every once in a while Carmen would stop and hug Jaz to her as if she, too, could see how unhappy Jaz appeared.

This thing between them had gone on long enough. Screw Seth and screw acting like a dickhead. He didn't want to distance himself from Jaz. He'd spent the last few days analyzing his feelings, analyzing goddamn everything, and enough was enough. The last thing he wanted to do was drive Jaz away or make her unhappy.

He strode forward into the kitchen to where Jaz was sitting. As she looked up in surprise, he gathered her in his arms and gave her a big hug. Then he dropped a kiss on her upturned lips. She blinked in shock, and he smiled at her reaction.

He brushed his thumb across the smudges beneath her eyes. "You look tired, Jaz." He cupped her cheeks and pulled her face to his again so he could kiss her. Her lips were deliciously soft against his, and he swallowed her sigh of contentment, held it close to him as he did her. He felt an odd sense of satisfaction, as if the decision he'd made had brought him peace.

He let her go and gently tucked her hair behind her ears. "Get some rest today and let Carmen take care of you. I'll be out with Seth for most of the day, but I'll see you when I get back."

Unable to resist one more taste, he brushed his lips across hers. He touched her cheek with his fingers then turned to walk out to where Seth waited.

Jasmine watched him go and wondered if she was having some bizarre dream. She raised her fingers to touch her tingling lips.

Carmen looked at her with a smug smile. "Maybe he is coming around, eh *niña?*"

"Maybe," she murmured.

What had gotten into him? Not that she was complaining. After Seth's rejection, one of the many that had been piling up lately, she'd spent the night in restless despair.

"What is wrong, Jasmine?" Carmen asked quietly. "You are not yourself today. You look sad."

Jasmine sighed. *Sad.* She wasn't sure that word covered it. Carmen wrapped her arms around her and hugged her to her ample bosom, and Jasmine clung to her, needing the comfort she offered.

Carmen stroked her back and murmured in Spanish near her ear. Several long minutes later, Carmen pulled away to look at her.

"What has happened, *niña?* You can talk to me, you know."

With little hesitation, Jasmine poured out the entire story, detailing the events of the last night and Seth's reaction. Carmen sat on the stool next to Jasmine, a look of sympathy creasing her round face.

"You weren't prepared for your first time."

Jasmine shook her head, embarrassed to admit her naivety. She wasn't ignorant of sex. She'd done plenty of experimentation and more than a little observation. But she had been caught off guard by what had happened last night.

Carmen sighed. "The first time is often painful, and if not painful, it's certainly not comfortable. It would have been better, I think, if he had known. There is much a man can do to make it easier for a woman if he knows and can prepare for it."

"Yes, but if he had known, he never would have touched me," Jasmine said ruefully.

Carmen nodded. "You are probably right."

"I don't know how to make him love me, *mamacita*. Maybe I never will. I love him and Zane so much. I don't want to imagine not being with them."

"Well, it would seem you're making progress with at least one of them," Carmen pointed out.

"It sounds greedy and selfish and manipulative," Jasmine began. "But I love them both so much that I cannot imagine a life without them both. As much as I love Zane, I'm not sure I could ever be with him with Seth on the outside, always there but not. The same goes for Seth. I couldn't be with him without Zane. So much rides on their acceptance of that fact," she said glumly. "Before I came home, I was so sure of myself. I imagined it would be easy to bowl them over. It's easy to think of how things will go when you're so far removed from the reality."

Carmen smiled. "You are very honest, *niña*. That's a start. Admitting your shortsightedness."

"Oh, I have no problem admitting my many faults," Jasmine said wryly.

Carmen patted her lovingly on the hand. "I've never known you to give up, *niña*. I don't always agree with your methods, and I've not completely approved of what it is you want now, but I know you have a pure heart and that you love those boys. And that is the most important thing. So if you love them, you mustn't give up. Love is worth fighting for."

Yes, Seth and Zane were worth fighting for. Jasmine just hoped that in the end she wasn't defeated.

Seth surveyed the freshly seeded food plots with satisfaction. He and Zane had worked all day to get the seed in the ground after the rain and in time for the next expected rain tonight.

He'd pushed himself hard, working through lunch, barely stopping for a drink. He was punishing himself, and he knew it, but he couldn't get last night out of his mind.

He'd hurt her, and he didn't know if he could forgive himself for that. He'd broken every oath he'd ever made to himself ever since she'd come into his life. A man's promise was everything, and if he couldn't keep his word to himself, then how could he be expected to be honorable with anyone else?

In all of it, though, he wasn't the angriest over his broken vow. No, what pissed him off the most was the fact that what he wanted was to go back to her and make it up to her. To love her as gently and as tenderly as he could. Show her how it could be instead of the rough, uncaring ass he'd shown himself to be the night before. He still cringed when he remembered the small whimper of pain when he'd driven ruthlessly into her.

God almighty. He closed his eyes, willing the memory away.

"Looks like we're done," Zane said as he tore off his gloves and tossed them into the back of the truck.

Seth nodded but didn't say anything. Zane seemed different today. More calm, less brooding and angry. He wasn't sure why, and he didn't really want to ask.

How would Zane react if he knew what had happened in Seth's bedroom last night? And why the hell had Zane and Jasmine been wrapped up in each other's arms if they hadn't had sex? He knew he owed Zane an apology but damned if he could offer him one without going into the details of how he knew Zane hadn't had sex with her.

"You want to run into Tucker's and get a drink?" Seth asked. "Maybe we'll run into Mary Jo." He said the last with a half-hearted smile and even less enthusiasm. Mary Jo hadn't been out to the ranch in nearly a year. The last time had been just a few weeks after Jasmine had left for Paris. Even then he hadn't been into it. Zane had driven her back to town because Seth hadn't wanted her to stay over.

Now as he looked at his brother, he knew Zane wasn't any more interested now than Seth had been then. Zane shook his head. "You go on without me. I'd rather hang out at the ranch tonight. I haven't spent much time with Jaz lately."

There was a subtle challenge to Zane's voice as if he expected Seth to object, but Seth stayed silent. He knew Jasmine and Zane had always been close, and it was apparent that Seth had seriously misjudged their relationship.

Seth walked toward the truck but paused as he opened the door. He stared over the hood at Zane who was getting into the passenger seat. "I'm sorry, man."

Zane met his gaze across the truck. "Me too."

They slid into the truck, and Seth knew it wouldn't be brought up again. Fighting with his brother wasn't one of his prouder moments, and he'd needed Zane to know it was something he regretted.

As they drove over the bumpy terrain back to the dirt road, Zane stared out the windshield. "Dad would be proud of what we've done with the place."

Seth looked at him in surprise. It had been a long while since they'd discussed their parents. He knew it was still a source of discomfort for Zane. Their deaths had affected him deeply.

"Yeah, I think he would. It was always his dream. He loved the land. Loved wildlife even more."

Zane smiled. "Do you remember the time we all went hunting in Alabama and Mom bagged a bigger buck than Dad?"

Seth chuckled. "Sure do. The old man was impossible to live with for a month after."

"He was proud of her, though. He bragged about her to anyone who would listen."

"That he did."

"I miss them," Zane said simply.

It grew quiet in the cab. "Yeah, so do I," Seth said finally.

It had been fourteen years since the tragic accident. At eighteen, Seth had just graduated high school and had been ready to go away to college. But he'd hung all that up to stay on the ranch and take care of his fourteen-year-old brother. Those first years had been tough. Not so much financially. Their parents had left them well provided for. But the brothers had been grief-stricken. Zane especially had been at an awkward age where he'd needed his parents. Seth had done the best he could to be both brother and parent, but he knew he hadn't measured up.

After they'd brought Jasmine home and hired Carmen, a sense of family had been restored to the ranch. It hadn't seemed as lonely. And when Jasmine had gone away, she'd taken a lot of the life with her. It wasn't the same without her.

But now that she'd come back, nothing would ever be as it was before. It was a complicated mess.

They drove the rest of the way to the ranch in silence. When Seth parked the truck, he and Zane got out to unhook the trailer and put away the equipment.

"Have a good time at Tucker's," Zane said as they made their way to the house. Zane stripped off his shirt and bundled it in a wad. He tossed it down in the laundry room on their way in. "I'm going to head up for a shower. I'll catch you when you get home."

Seth nodded as he kicked off his boots. Carmen would have his ass if he tracked dirt on her floors. He pulled off his shirt but stopped short of taking his pants off. In the past, he wouldn't have hesitated, but now it didn't seem appropriate. Damn shame when a man couldn't walk through his own house in his underwear.

He walked barefooted through the kitchen and into the living room. As he started for the stairs, he met Jasmine at the bottom. She ducked her head and looked away but not before he saw the hurt in her eyes and the smudges underneath.

His chest tightened uncomfortably as she walked away. He'd give anything to have last night back again. He'd give anything not to have hurt her. But he'd done nothing but hurt her ever since she'd returned. It seemed to be the one thing he was good at lately.

With a soft curse, he trudged up the stairs to his bathroom. He needed to be away for the evening, and he had no intention of looking up Mary Jo, or any other woman for that matter. What he could use were a few stiff drinks and a bottle of you-fucked-up.

Chapter Sixteen

It was just as well that Seth had left. If Zane had to guess, he'd be gone damn near all night. He had that dark look that meant he was brooding about something, and when that happened, he usually threw back a few and slept it off in town.

Jaz was in her room, and he hadn't heard a peep from her all evening. As ridiculous as it sounded, Zane was nervous about going to her. He knew he'd hurt her with his brush-off and subsequent avoidance. She might not be in a very receptive mood.

But he had to address this thing between them. He had to do something to assuage the constant ache. It wasn't just sexual either. His chest hurt half the time and the other half he felt strangely empty.

He stood outside of Jaz's room and tapped lightly on her door. When he heard her soft call to come in, he pushed the door open and stepped around it.

She was sitting on the bed, her back propped against the half dozen pillows she insisted on sleeping with. She was wearing only a thin T-shirt that touched the top of her navel and a pair of lacy panties.

When she met his gaze, her cheeks became a dusty pink, and she grabbed for the covers. "I thought you were Carmen."

He said nothing. He walked over to the bed, sat down on the edge and drew one leg up so he was turned toward her.

"I've missed you, Jaz," he said simply.

He reached out a hand to touch her cheek. Her eyes closed briefly as if she found pleasure in his gesture. He stroked his fingers over her skin and pulled her hair away from her face to tuck it behind her ear.

"I've missed you too," she whispered.

Slowly he lowered his head, closing the distance between them. He slid his hand behind her neck until his palm cradled the base of her skull. He pulled her to him to meet his kiss.

A soft sigh escaped her, and he felt a tremor work its way through her body.

"I want you, Jaz. I've argued with myself. I swore I wouldn't touch you, but at the moment, I can't think of a single reason why I can't make love to you."

As she pulled further away, he could see shadows in her eyes. The sight did funny things to his heart. He wanted her to shine. He wanted to make her light up. It was only now that he realized just how much his rejection had hurt her.

"I won't push you away again, honey," he murmured as he trailed a finger down the line of her jaw.

She sighed heavily. "There are things you need to know, Zane. I have to be honest with you. I can't hide the truth from you anymore."

Jasmine watched as he processed her statement with a look of wariness. He glanced uncertainly at her.

"What do you need to tell me?" he asked cautiously.

His hand paused in its descent, and she reached up to cup it, wanting to touch him in some way. She wasn't sure how he would take her revelation. She wasn't really ready to tell him, but if he was here for why she thought, she couldn't allow matters to go further without him knowing everything.

Zane appreciated bluntness. He wasn't much into games or long, drawn-out dramas so the longer she pussyfooted around the issue, the more annoyed he'd become.

"I slept with Seth last night."

Zane blinked in surprise. "Slept? As in slept like you do sometimes in my bed or are we talking about something else?"

"As in I was a virgin when you and I had sex, and then I had sex with Seth. He was my first. Well, technically you were my first," she corrected and groaned inwardly at the mess she was making of things. "He was the first I had actual intercourse with."

Zane's hand fell away from her face, and he dragged it through his hair, a look of confusion marring his features.

"But why? I mean I noticed that things weren't good between you and Seth, but I assumed it was because of what happened between you and me."

If she didn't make him understand and understand soon, she was going to lose him before she ever got her mouth open. She leaned forward, curling her feet underneath her so she pressed into his chest. He was stiff against her.

She moved her hands up his body, and then she cupped his face between her palms. "I love you, Zane."

He looked even more confused by her declaration.

"But I love Seth, too."

Understanding flickered in his eyes, something she hadn't expected.

He reached up and took one of her hands from his face. He turned it over and pressed his lips to her palm. "What happened with Seth?"

"He was furious with me," she admitted. "I snuck into his room and seduced him. Things were good until he realized I was a virgin. Then he got pissed and we didn't finish. He hasn't spoken to me since."

"Does he know you love him...me?"

"I told him I loved him. I haven't told him I love you. He won't accept that I love him, so I can't imagine he'd take the news that I love you both any better."

Zane sighed. "We've both hurt you badly."

"I haven't handled it well." She shrugged. "What was I supposed to do? I don't always understand it myself. There aren't any rule books for something like this."

She studied his face, looking for disgust, anger, anything to let her know that she'd just lost any chance of earning his love. But all she saw was the same understanding she'd seen earlier.

"Does it make you angry?" she asked hesitantly.

His lips twisted, and he gave a little shrug. "To be honest, I'm not sure how I feel. I suppose I should be angry. Jealous even. But I can also understand how you have feelings for us both."

He studied her for a long moment. "What is it that you want, Jaz? Because I want you happy above all else."

She hesitated, gathering her courage and praying that what she was about to say wouldn't drive him away.

"What if I told you that the only way I could be happy is if I was with you both. If you both loved me and were willing to accept that I loved you both?"

She saw an odd mixture of relief as well as something else she couldn't quite name in his eyes.

"You're not holding out for which of us makes a move first?" he asked gruffly.

She was a little stung by the question even though she recognized how it must look. What she was proposing wasn't everyday run-of-the-mill.

"I love you both," she said simply. "I want...I want a life with both of you. It's why I came home. Is that something you can accept?"

She regretted the question. It was too soon. She hadn't given him time, and she shouldn't be pressuring him.

"I don't know," he said honestly. "I came to you tonight because I wanted you in my arms. I wanted to make love to you. I wasn't prepared—"

She put a finger over his lips to shush him. "Then love me," she said softly. "Everything else can wait."

Chapter Seventeen

Zane looked at Jasmine with hungry eyes. Her heart fluttered and rolled as he leaned in to kiss her. His hands cupped her face, and his thumbs brushed across her cheek bones as his tongue found hers.

He pushed forward, leaning her back until she settled against the pillows. He kissed her lovingly, so gently, her chest swelled and ached.

His hands skated down her body until they reached her hips. He lifted his weight off her long enough to pull her down the bed until she was lying flat on the mattress.

He settled above her, looking down with fierce eyes. "Did he hurt you, Jaz?"

She swallowed at the concern in his voice. "It was my first time. Carmen said if he had known, he could have made it better for me."

"I'll take care of you, baby," he murmured, his words a promise that brushed across her skin, a caress she felt to her soul.

He lowered his dark head to kiss her belly. His hands inched up from their grip on her hips. He inserted his fingers under the band of her T-shirt and pulled, the soft material rubbing across her taut nipples.

He emitted a sound of male satisfaction when her breasts bobbed free of the shirt. He yanked it the rest of the way over her head and tossed it to the floor.

For a long moment, he cradled her there in his arms just looking at her. He nudged her legs open and settled his big body between them, his head positioned at her ribcage.

He pressed soft, tender kisses to her belly and up and down the ridge of her ribs. She shivered as his tongue lapped at the underswell of her breast. It moved closer to her nipple until finally, the bud balanced on the end of his tongue. He let it rest there for a moment before sucking it strongly between his teeth.

She arched into him with a cry.

He continued to suck with rhythmic motions as he reached down to tug at her panties. She elevated her hips in an effort to help him.

He released her nipple for a moment as he pulled the underwear free of her legs. She couldn't help the sigh of disappointment.

He chuckled and glanced back up at her, his eyes fiery with desire. "Don't worry, baby. I'm not going anywhere. I plan to give you everything you could possibly want and more."

Her pussy clenched as his words sent lust blazing through her core. "I want *you*," she said simply.

"You'll have me."

Their gazes met, and she saw promise in his eyes. Determination. Did this mean he was okay with all she'd told him? For now, she didn't want to dwell on it. What she wanted most was to be in his arms, his body over hers, him driving into her, making her his. God, she wanted to be his. She'd spent so long dreaming about this moment.

She reached for him, wanting him, all of him. He went willingly into her arms, and she held him close as his muscled body covered hers.

He kissed her neck and nibbled at the sensitive skin. He nipped at her ears, sucked at the lobes, alternating between the two.

She could feel his hardness cradled between her legs, her pussy cupping him. She wasn't afraid. She hadn't been afraid of Seth, just unprepared. She widened her legs and curled them around his body, wanting him inside her.

"No baby, not yet," he murmured in her ear. "You're not ready."

She moaned. "Yes, I am."

He chuckled again. "No, you're not. But you will be before I'm through."

He began to slide down her body, slowly, showering kisses as he made his way down. He stopped at her breasts and gave each equal attention. He lapped at the buds and sucked them until she was restless and aching with need. But he didn't stop there.

He moved lower to her belly and traced the area around her navel. He played with her belly ring for a while before he finally pressed tiny kisses down to her pelvis.

He placed his head between her legs and kissed the insides of both thighs. With an impatient nudge, he pushed her legs further apart so that her pussy was completely bared to him.

"Please," she whispered.

He parted her folds with a gentle finger and then pressed his tongue to her opening. Her hips convulsed as tiny spasms radiated from her pelvis.

He licked upward, and she jumped again when the tip of his tongue slid across her clit. He lapped repeatedly, working the quivering button into a firestorm of sensation. He swirled around and over then sucked it into his mouth to tease her some more.

"I've dreamed of tasting you again. You're like an addiction. After that first time, I could think of nothing else. I can't wait to feel that sweet heat surrounding my dick, can't wait to lose myself in you, baby."

She closed her eyes as his words enveloped her like a safety net protecting her from the rest of the world. Nothing could hurt her here, in his arms.

He slid a finger inside her. "You're so small. I don't want to hurt you, but God, I can't wait to be inside you."

"Don't make me wait any longer." She reached for him, wanting him close, wanting him a part of her.

He moved up her body and settled between her legs, one hand gently spreading her in preparation. He found her entrance and eased inside, the broad head stretching the delicate tissues.

His fingers moved upward to stroke at her clit as he eased further in. She gripped him tighter and wrapped her legs around his waist, locking him against her.

"You're not hurting me," she whispered. "You feel magnificent."

He let out a tortured groan and stilled for a moment. He worked his hand free and placed both arms on the mattress on either side of her head.

As he rocked forward, she let out a gasp of pleasure as he slid all the way into her body. He lowered his head to hers and kissed her lips as he began moving in and out.

"I love you, Jaz."

Slowly, so tenderly, with such exquisite care, he thrust between her legs. Each stroke was measured, and she felt each one to her very soul.

A delicious coil of tension began wrapping in her pussy, spreading to her belly. Tighter and tighter until she feared bursting. It was a slow climb to something fantastic, nothing like the quick orgasms of the past. Each time she thought she'd surely fall over the edge, she merely climbed higher, and the tension grew until she writhed in Zane's arms, helpless against the pleasure he was giving her.

"Come for me, baby," he whispered. "I want to watch you come in my arms, feel you tighten around me."

She shuddered as another tiny spasm sent her higher. She closed her eyes, but he kissed her lids. "Open them. I want to see you," he said.

Her eyes flashed open just as her orgasm broke and flooded around her. Her mouth fell open as a soundless cry emerged. She wanted to scream, but couldn't. "Oh God," she gasped.

"That's it. Let go. I've got you."

Her pussy throbbed and pulsed. She tightened her legs around his waist and gripped his shoulders, her fingers digging into his muscles.

He picked up his pace and thrust more forcefully into her, as if recognizing it was what she needed.

The room blurred and Zane went out of focus. She could hear the slap of his thighs meeting her flesh. She could feel him deep inside her, a connection she never imagined she could feel so intensely.

He murmured his love for her. She held him as she came down from the clouds. Her body finally relaxed and she melted into the bed.

Still, she could feel him thrusting, now more gently. Then he stiffened over her, and he gripped her just as tightly as she held him.

"I want to watch you," she whispered, echoing his earlier desire.

His gaze found hers, and she could see the strain on his face, the sheer ecstasy in his eyes. Sweat beaded his forehead. His jaw clenched. His eyes seemed to explode in a myriad of emotions just as his body did the same.

He collapsed around her, his chest heaving as he tried to catch up. He buried his face in the curve of her neck and peppered tiny kisses to her skin.

After several long seconds, he propped himself on his arms and lifted himself off her just a bit. He stared down at her, lazy contentment shining in his eyes. His fingers trailed down her cheek and tucked loose strands of her hair behind her ears. Uncertainty flickered across his face as he studied her.

"Did I hurt you?"

She shook her head and reached up to touch his jaw. "It was wonderful," she said, emotion knotting her throat.

He rolled to the side and cradled her in his arms. She snuggled into his chest and sighed with contentment. Things were almost perfect. They would be if she knew where she stood with Seth.

Zane must have sensed the change in her, because he pulled away and looked down at her. "What's wrong?"

Instead of simply saying she'd been thinking of Seth, she turned to the other concern weighing on her.

"Are you upset that I slept with Seth? Most people would look at a situation like this and think I was a royal tramp."

He frowned. "I don't give a shit what other people think, Jaz."

He blew out his breath and rolled to his back to stare up at the ceiling. She rose up on her elbow so she could look at him.

"You didn't answer the question."

He reached out with his hand to caress her back, his hand sliding up and down her spine. His fingers caught her hair, and he played with the ends.

"I'm being honest here, Jaz. I'm not entirely sure how I feel yet. What you suggest...well, it's a little hard to swallow. On some level, I'm not surprised that you have feelings for both of us. I can understand how and why. I mean the three of us have lived together and been through good times and bad over the last six years. But the other part of me...that part of me is relieved to know that you love me and want to be with me. I don't want to imagine my life without you. I think if I have that reassurance I can come to terms with the idea that I might have to share...you...with my brother."

He looked strangely vulnerable, as if he was worried his confession would somehow lessen him in her eyes. She leaned forward, her heart in her throat. She laid her head on his chest and wrapped her arms around his neck, hugging him as tight as she could.

"I love you," she whispered fiercely. "I've always loved you."

He stroked her back and kissed the top of her head. "I love you, too, Jaz. I'm so glad you're home."

"Make love to me again. I've waited so long for you."

His hands tightened on her. "We didn't use protection, Jaz. I'm not worried about disease and shit, but I don't want to get you pregnant. Not yet."

She smiled and rose up to look at him. "I'm taking birth control."

His eyes reflected relief. "Don't get me wrong, Jaz. The idea of your belly swelling with my baby...that's some seriously heady stuff, but you're too young, and we've got too much to work out without adding to it."

Her stomach turned over, and she wanted to burst with the joy she felt.

"You don't think you're too old for me anymore?" she asked mischievously.

"Old? Hell, I'm only six years older than you. That doesn't make me ancient, I hope."

She leaned down to kiss him. "It makes you perfect."

Chapter Eighteen

Seth let himself in the dark house and closed the door behind him. He was careful not to wake anyone as he climbed the stairs toward his room.

He stopped by Zane's room, intending to talk to his brother, but he found it empty, the bed not yet slept in. He frowned as he turned to stare in the direction of Jasmine's closed door.

He shook his head at his paranoia. He'd been wrong before about Zane's involvement with Jasmine. Yet, he found himself walking down the hall, pausing outside her room.

Quietly and carefully, he turned the knob, not wanting to wake her up if she was asleep. He cracked the door and saw soft light from a bedside lamp. He pushed an inch more and froze when he saw Zane's naked body between Jasmine's legs. He was arching into her, and Seth could hear her soft moans of pleasure.

He should turn away, but he was riveted by the scene. He felt like a seedy voyeur. Actually, he felt a lot of things. Anger, betrayal, and arousal.

To his never-ending shame, what he really wanted to do was join them. Slide his cock into her luscious mouth while Zane took her from behind.

He closed his eyes against the erotic image of Jasmine between them. A place he'd sworn she'd never be. Not her.

Never her. She wasn't a cheap plaything for his and Zane's amusement.

His fingers tight around the knob, he backed away from the alluring sight before him. He shut the door, careful not to make a sound. As he started back down the hall, he cursed the fact that, for all practical purposes, he'd become a peeping Tom in his own home.

As soon as he entered his bedroom, he let the anger that had crept over him take firmer hold. How could she have crawled from his bed to his brother's? She'd been a virgin, and yet she was acting little better than a whore.

He cringed even as the word crossed his mind. Jasmine was no whore. He had no right to judge her. But the fact remained that she'd gone straight from his bed to Zane's. What game was she playing?

Or maybe he'd hurt her so much that she'd found solace in a more willing partner. He'd acted badly, ignored her then taken her rough and hard, no way for him to ever treat her. In that light he certainly couldn't blame her for seeking tenderness elsewhere.

His head ached, but his thoughts returned repeatedly to what he knew was taking place just down the hall. How could he sleep when Zane was making Jasmine his a room away?

With an irritated growl, he yanked his door open and headed back downstairs. He should have done what he'd originally planned and just gotten a hotel room in town. Then he would have never come home to see Zane between Jasmine's legs and in her arms. A place that, if he would admit it, he very much wanted to be.

℃

Before she'd drifted off to sleep the night before, Jasmine had been afraid that when she woke the next morning, Zane would be gone. But his arms were wound tightly around her, and her nose was pressed to his hard chest.

She lay there for several minutes soaking it in. It was almost too much to comprehend. What she'd wanted for so long, had ached for the last six years, was finally hers.

For the first time since her arrival, she felt as though she'd truly come home.

He stirred against her, and his hands trailed through her hair. She snuggled further into him, not wanting the moment to end.

"Good morning," he murmured.

She pulled her head back and kissed him. "I love you." She couldn't help but say it again. She wanted to say it over and over and hear him say it in return. It was what she'd wanted to hear forever, it seemed.

"I love you, too, Jaz. Believe that, okay?"

She smiled. He seemed to know she needed reassurance.

He touched her cheek and stroked his fingers over her jaw repeatedly. "How do you plan to lay this out to Seth?"

She sucked in her breath. "I don't know," she said in a low voice. "He was so angry with me after what happened the other night."

Zane looked curiously at her. "What exactly did you do?"

Her cheeks warmed. "I borrowed handcuffs from J.T. and handcuffed Seth to his bed. Then I stripped in front of him and seduced him."

"I'm guessing he didn't fight you too hard," Zane said dryly.

"He was reluctant. At first. But then..." She sighed. "It hurt, and I didn't expect it. I know that sounds stupid. I'm not stupid about sex, and uhm, I've experimented with alternative measures to the full-blown act of sex, all of which I enjoyed, so I honestly didn't think it would feel so...well...terrible!"

"He wouldn't have liked hurting you," Zane said gruffly.

She shook her head. "No, he didn't. I know he hated it. And on the heels of that, he hated me for forcing the issue. He was angry that I didn't tell him. I should have, I suppose, but he wouldn't have touched me if he knew I was still a virgin."

"And why were you?" Zane asked softly. "You've not had a shortage of men interested in you despite our best efforts to beat the shit out of all of them."

She grinned but then sobered as his stare penetrated her. "Two reasons. One, I couldn't imagine giving myself willingly to anyone but you and Seth. And two, after what happened six years ago, when I was expected to sell myself for sex...I swore I'd always value my body and my self-respect more than that. I wouldn't give my body to anyone I didn't love."

Zane squeezed her to him and kissed her forehead. "I don't know what to tell you about Seth, baby. I'm not even sure what I want to happen. I won't lie to you. But I'm not angry about what happened between you. I understand what it is you want, and while I'm not convinced it's what I want, we'll work it out. I don't want to lose you. If you believe nothing else, believe that I won't let you go."

Her heart took wings and flew at his vow. "Thank you," she whispered. "For understanding."

He kissed her again then pulled away with a look of regret. "We should go downstairs. It's late, and while I don't mind who knows it, we should ease Carmen into this. It's going to be a hard adjustment for her. She still sees you very much as her baby. Not to mention the fact that Seth is going to want to kick my ass again."

Her eyes flew to his. "You won't fight again, will you?" she asked anxiously. "I don't want to come between you. I love you too much."

He smiled as she touched the fading bruise around his eye. "We won't fight, baby. And if we do, it's nothing for you to worry about. We've squabbled since we were children. It's what brothers do. Now hop up and let's go get breakfast before Carmen comes and chases us out of bed."

They dressed and headed downstairs together. Carmen eyed them suspiciously as they sat down to eat.

"You two are speaking again, eh?" she observed as she puttered around, setting plates in front of them.

"Yes, *mamacita*," Jasmine said with a smile.

"We're doing more than talking," Zane said with a wink in Carmen's direction.

"Zane!" Jasmine exclaimed, shocked that he'd be so blunt.

Carmen chuckled and shook her head. "This girl is impossible to resist when she puts her mind to something, yes?"

Zane grinned. "Yes."

Carmen stepped between them and pulled them both into a hug. "I'm very happy for both of you. I love you both as my own."

"Where is Seth this morning?" Jasmine asked casually as Carmen walked back toward the stove.

Carmen turned, her gaze troubled. "He hasn't come home."

Zane shrugged. "He was heading to Tucker's last night. You know him. If he drank, he'd stay in the hotel."

"But it isn't like him to drink so much that he can't drive," Jasmine murmured.

"He's upset right now, Jaz. You have to give him some time. He's got a lot on his mind."

She nodded unhappily. She was impatient. Now that things appeared to be working out between her and Zane, she was more anxious than ever to bring Seth into the relationship. But even as she thought it, she realized it would be the battle of her life.

As if sensing her dour thoughts, Zane leaned forward and wrapped his arms around her. "Just give him time, honey. That's all you can do."

Chapter Nineteen

Jasmine's wait for Seth to return bordered on a sick vigil. She paced the living room and haunted the window overlooking the driveway. Zane had gone out to do some work, a fact she was grateful for, because she didn't want to have the confrontation with Seth when Zane was present.

Supper was a subdued affair. Jasmine sat and picked at her food while Zane wolfed down his. Even Carmen didn't have much to say. After they'd eaten, Zane dropped a kiss on her forehead.

"I'm going to go up and grab a shower and head to bed. I'll see you...later," he said.

Jasmine nodded and smiled, though it was a strain to do so. The longer she waited for Seth to come home, the more worried and anxious she became.

She stood by the window long after darkness fell, staring down the road. Finally around midnight, she saw the headlights of his truck bounce over the hill. She stepped away from the window and rubbed her hands nervously down the back of her jeans.

When she heard the slam of his truck door, she changed her mind about talking to him here, and she headed for the stairs. She raced up and hurried down to his bedroom. She let herself in and sat down on the edge of his bed to wait, her heart thudding in sick worry.

She didn't have long to wait. He must have come straight to his room because the door opened just a few moments later. He didn't see her immediately, but when he shut the door and turned his gaze toward her, it hardened, and he frowned.

"What do you want?" he demanded.

She flinched at the harshness of his tone, but she wouldn't be cowed. This was too important.

"I need to talk to you, Seth. Please."

His expression wavered. Then he studied her closer, and concern flashed in his eyes. "Are you all right? Is something wrong?"

She sighed. No matter how angry he might be with her, it was obvious he still cared about her on some level. The question was on which one? As a sister? Or a woman?

"I wanted to talk about the other night," she said hesitantly.

He shut himself off from her, his eyes growing cold and hard. She shivered and nearly lost her courage in that moment.

"You want to talk about the other night, Jasmine?" His voice was quiet, too soft, dangerously so. "Oh, we can talk about it. Right after you tell me why you went straight from my bed into Zane's."

She blanched. Surely Zane hadn't told him. Which only meant one thing. He must have seen them.

"I saw you," he confirmed. "Saw Zane between your legs. You weren't acting the innocent virgin then."

She flushed and ducked her head.

"What game are you playing?" he asked. "I won't let you come between me and my brother."

155

She shook her head sadly. "What have I ever done to make you think so badly of me, Seth? I never want to come between you and Zane. I love you. I love you both."

Seth's eyes narrowed in confusion.

She stood and walked toward him. Seth backed away a step, but she didn't stop.

"I love you, Seth. I've always loved you. But I love Zane, too. I love you both with all my heart."

"What are you saying, Jasmine?" Seth asked in a voice rife with incredulity.

She sighed. "I know it sounds crazy. It took me a long time to come to terms with it. But the fact is, I love you both. I don't want to be without either of you. It's why I left and why I came back. Because I decided to fight for you instead of giving up before I ever tried."

Seth ran a hand through his short black hair, and a whole host of emotions ran through his blue eyes. Some of which she didn't want to see there. Anger. Pity. Especially pity.

"I don't even know what to say," he muttered.

"You've shared women before," she pointed out. "I watched you with Mary Jo," she said in a lower voice. "I wanted to be her so badly. I was jealous. Still am. And there were other women."

Seth's mouth popped open, and then his entire face softened. He put a hand on Jasmine's shoulder and guided her toward the bed. He sat beside her and touched her on the cheek.

"Jasmine, honey, listen to me. That's not the same."

She arched an eyebrow. "Isn't it?"

He sighed and rubbed a hand over his face. "Yes, Zane and I have had sex with the same woman. At the same time." His voice sounded oddly strangled. "But it's a kink. One we both enjoy. Some women enjoy threesomes. I've shared a woman with…with someone other than Zane as well. It's not the same as what you suggest. I may share a woman during sex, but I will never share a woman I care about with another man. Even my brother."

"Are you saying I have to make a choice between you and Zane?" she asked, her horror growing with each second. Her heart pounded so hard, she could feel each beat, each sickening pulse.

Seth shook his head. "No, honey, I wouldn't make you make that choice. I'm making it for you. A relationship between us, you and me, is impossible. The other night…was a mistake. I should have never touched you."

Her face felt frozen. The tears she wanted to shed were locked under ice. She stared at him, her hopes and dreams cracking under the weight of her despair.

"It could work," she whispered. "Maybe I misunderstood the times you had sex with the same woman, but there is no reason it couldn't work on a permanent basis. I don't want a threesome. I could get that anywhere. I'm not looking for some sexual kink or thrill. I love you. I love you both, and I want a life with both of you. How is that so wrong?"

"Because you're asking me to do something I can't do," Seth said hoarsely.

She stared at him, completely numb. "And maybe you just don't love me enough," she whispered. She rose from the bed, unable to keep looking at him, not when she wanted so much to be in his arms. She wanted him to erase the hurt and rejection of the other night, and instead she'd been handed another rejection.

"I love you, Seth. I'll always love you. I can't accept a life here with Zane if you aren't a part of it."

She turned and walked away from him. He never made a sound as she walked into the hallway and shut his door behind her.

Chapter Twenty

Zane was awake when his door eased open. He hadn't been able to sleep despite telling Jaz he was beat. How could he have slept when she was down the hall with Seth?

And now she was standing in his doorway. Even in the darkness he could tell she was upset, unsure of herself.

"Come here, baby," he murmured.

She hurried to his bed, and when he held his arms up to her, she climbed in and threw herself against his chest. He held her close as he felt her tremble against him.

His insides twisted, and his feelings were a mass of confusion. He should be happy. Jaz was his, or at least partly his. She loved him, and he loved her. He hated that her happiness was not entirely in his hands, but at the same time he understood her need for both him and Seth. It was a damn helpless feeling and one he didn't like at all.

What kind of a sick fuck did it make him to stand by while she went to his brother? Strangely, that didn't bother him. What bothered him was the fact that Jaz was crying in his arms, and he was powerless to make her stop.

He rolled until she was nestled against his side. Then he cupped her cheek with his palm and lowered his lips to kiss her.

"Let me love you," he whispered.

He didn't know what else to do, how else to show her that things would work out. He couldn't make that promise, anyway. All he could do was make her believe that no matter what happened with Seth, he wouldn't leave her.

She reached for him, hot, needy, her mouth claiming his. This was Jaz, his Jaz. In some ways she'd always belonged to him just as she'd always belonged to Seth. Perhaps that was why he was okay with the idea of Seth holding a part of her heart. She'd been theirs ever since they'd brought her home six years ago. She'd filled a hole in their hearts left barren by their parents' deaths. She brought sunshine and warmth to a ranch that had been cold for so many years. And he'd waited for her to grow up. Had even let her go, but somehow he'd always known she'd return.

He slid her jeans down her legs, touching her silken skin on the way, his hands caressing, loving. After he tossed the jeans aside, his hands traveled back up until his thumbs hooked into the thin strap of her panties. His other hand tugged her shirt higher as he pushed his palm up her spine, his fingers splayed across her back.

She kissed his neck, and he shivered as chills chased each other down his back. Her small tongue flicked out to lick at the skin just below his ear, and then she sucked his earring into her mouth.

He pushed impatiently at her panties then moved his hand from her back to the curve of her ass. She had a perfect behind. Firm, well-rounded.

He scooted down in the bed until his mouth was even with her side. As he pulled her underwear the rest of the way down her legs, he kissed the rounded swell of her hip.

He pushed her over until she lay on her back. He looked up at her to see her staring at him, her eyes full of need and desire. Whatever had gone on with Seth, Zane knew that in this moment she wasn't thinking of his brother. All he could see in her eyes was himself.

"I love you," he said, knowing she needed his reassurance, and the truth was, he couldn't get enough of telling her. Maybe it reassured him as well, reminded him that she was here in his arms.

"Make me yours," she whispered, an emotional catch to her voice. It was husky, the sound turning his heart over and clenching his chest tight.

He slid his hand between her thighs and gently parted them. He leaned down and brushed his lips across the tiny curls covering her pussy.

He couldn't get enough of her taste, her smell. He wanted to dive into her sweetness and never come up for air. Wanted to lose himself in her liquid heat.

With two fingers, he parted her folds and licked at her entrance then up to her clit. She jerked beneath him, and he could feel spasms work through her legs.

He eased one finger inside her and moaned as her pussy sucked and clenched around it. She was so tight just around one finger. He stifled a groan as he remembered how that tightness had felt around his cock. His groin ached with the need to thrust into her. Impatience cut through him, slick like a razor blade and every bit as sharp.

She was wet, but not enough yet, and he didn't want to hurt her. Never.

He eased another finger inside and gently worked in and out as he sucked at her clit. He withdrew his fingers and slid his body up hers until his mouth was at her breasts. His fingers, still damp with her moisture, rubbed over one nipple and then the other, leaving a sweet trail around the buds.

Then he sucked one of his fingers into his mouth while she watched. Her eyes widened and flared in arousal. He held out the second finger to her, brushing it across her lips.

"Taste," he invited.

She hesitated as if unsure then slowly opened her mouth for his finger. He swiped it across her tongue then pulled against the suction of her lips until it popped free.

He bent and licked one nipple, tasting her arousal. He sucked it into his mouth, working it up and down with the force of his lips. Then he turned his attention to the other, giving it equal treatment.

"Please, I need you," she begged. "I want you inside me."

He lowered a hand to her pussy and eased a finger inside once more, wanting to see if she was prepared for him. Satisfied that she was, he spread her wider and positioned himself at her entrance.

She shifted impatiently underneath him but he held back, determined to set the pace. Slowly, torturously, he pushed inside her. A shudder worked over his body as she enveloped him, welcomed him, grasped him with her warmth.

He inched forward even though his body screamed at him to plunge deep, to ride her long and hard, make her his in the most primitive way a man could own a woman. But in fact, she owned him. Every piece of his heart and soul.

Finally she took matters into her own hands. She wrapped her legs around his hips and arched forward, taking him the rest of the way home.

He lowered himself, allowing her to take some of his weight but not all. He loved the feeling of her pressed to every inch of his skin. The contrast between her softness and the hardness of his body fascinated him. It gave him a sense of her trust. He could so easily crush her. Hurt her.

Her hands slipped over his shoulders, her fingers digging into him as he thrust into her. He could feel her quivering around him, her pussy gripping him, fluttering softly as her body tensed. She was close, and he was determined she'd get there first.

"My Jaz," he murmured. "My sweet Jaz."

She fused her lips to his, and he was swamped by the heady mixture of sweet and hot, love and lust.

She began to shake, and her legs and arms tightened around him. He thrust harder and reached down between them to stroke at her clit. She gasped and then latched onto his neck, burying her face in his shoulder.

He clenched his teeth and held himself still for a moment until he was sure she'd experienced her release. Then he let go, burying himself as deeply as he could go. He withdrew then thrust forward once, twice and finally again.

His balls tightened unbearably. Every muscle in his body clenched until he erupted deep inside her, the relief making him weak. He lay wedged within her, content to remain still as he jerked and finished inside her.

He gathered her to him and shifted until he was beside her. He stroked her hair and kissed the top of her head. "I love you," he said one more time.

She kissed his chest and snuggled deeper into his embrace. "I love you too, Zane. So much. And never less than Seth. I need you to know that."

Her words touched a worry that he didn't even know he'd had, but as she uttered them, he felt some of his anxiety lift. He squeezed her and let his hands wander over her, content to touch her.

"I know," he finally said. "I know, Jaz."

Chapter Twenty-One

Jasmine woke the next morning curled tight in Zane's arms. For a moment, she allowed herself to absorb the utter contentment she felt, but then she remembered the encounter with Seth the previous night.

It was an unwelcome jolt of reality.

Zane's lips brushed across her temple. "I have to go."

She turned to him. "Where?"

"San Antonio. Remember?"

She hadn't remembered. "How long will you be gone?"

"Just for the day. I'll be back late tonight." He paused for a minute then cupped her chin in his hand. "You could go with me."

She was tempted. It would take her away from the ranch and Seth for the day, but then that would defeat the purpose of her coming home in the first place. And what she really wanted was a few hours to wander over the land with her camera. It had always lifted her spirits in the past. Maybe she'd see Old Man again.

"I think I'm going to go out with my camera," she said. "I haven't been riding since I got back home. I doubt Esme even remembers me."

Zane rolled out of bed and strode naked to the door. He looked so graceful and comfortable in his skin. Long, sleek, dark and beautiful. His hair curled down his neck and touched the tops of his shoulders. The muscles in his back bunched and rippled as he pulled a shirt over his head.

When he'd finished dressing, he walked back over to the bed where she was now sitting up, holding the sheet to her chest with one hand. He bent and kissed her—long, hot, breathless.

"Think of me today."

She smiled. "I will."

She watched him go, and sighed heavily as the door closed a few seconds later. Her limbs heavy and lethargic, she swung her feet over the edge of the bed and stood. She trudged into the bathroom to take a long hot shower.

Twenty minutes, later, Jasmine walked through the kitchen, surprised to see Carmen nowhere in the vicinity. She laid her camera bag down on the counter and scribbled a quick note telling Carmen where she was going. She stuck it to the fridge with a magnet, collected her camera then headed out to the barn to saddle Esme.

She smiled when she passed Lucky and Tanner, Seth's and Zane's horses. She held out a hand to pet their noses before walking on to Esme's stall.

Just months after arriving at the ranch, Jasmine had gone horse mad. In an effort to indulge her and bring her out of her shell, they'd bought her Esme. But she hadn't wanted to ride alone, so they'd each gotten a horse so they could accompany her. It had become a favorite pastime of theirs, riding over the terrain in the evenings, deer watching.

"Hey girl," Jasmine whispered as Esme nuzzled her cheek. Esme whickered softly in return as Jasmine stroked her neck.

After saddling her, Jasmine led her outside the barn into the morning sun. She threw the strap of her camera bag over the pommel then pulled herself up into the saddle.

Her heart lightened as they disappeared into the back country of the ranch. The sun shone hot and unrelenting, and she relished every minute of it. She soaked in the rays, the land, the peace that surrounded her at the idea of being home.

She stopped at the usually dry river bed that now trickled with the remnants of the recent rain and let Esme drink while she took several shots of the jagged serpentine design cut into the sand and rock.

She loved the earthy colors, the smatterings of browns and oranges, deep reds and pale yellows. Every once in a while a jackrabbit would scare up and run balls to the wall across the ground only to disappear behind a clump of cacti.

Jasmine pushed her hair away from her face, the strands damp with sweat. She tucked her camera back into its case and swung back into the saddle. She led Esme away from the creek bed as the sun rose higher.

Home. The word, the feeling, echoed with every clop of Esme's hooves. Maybe it made her ridiculously sentimental, but never had she experienced such a feeling of homecoming. She'd never had a place where she belonged. Where she fit so well.

Now that feeling was threatened by Seth's resistance, his rejection of...she wouldn't say of her, because deep down, she didn't feel he was rejecting her. He was rejecting what she wanted. Her idea of their future.

She clung to that thought, to the hope that as long as there was something there between them, pulling them together, the rest would fall into place.

But how? She pressed her lips together in a thin line. Her head ached, a dull pounding working at her temples. She knew she'd been incredibly naïve in thinking that what she proposed would be accepted. Oh, she hadn't expected it to be easy, but in the back of her mind, she'd harbored fantasies of them realizing their love for her and not being willing to let her go.

She sighed. She had to face it. She hadn't seen beyond her selfish expectations. What she was asking...it wasn't fair. But then what about love was? She knew she was asking a lot. But it didn't change the fact that she truly loved both men. Deeply. Passionately. With all her heart. It wasn't a childish infatuation. It wasn't a crush that would go away with time. Whether it was fair or not, sane or insane, she loved them both, and she'd never, ever view either man as a "spare", an extra, in case the first didn't work out.

She shuddered at the idea that either would perceive the situation like that.

She loved them. Would always love them.

Distracted by the intensity of her thoughts, she allowed the reins too much slack. When a rabbit darted through Esme's legs, startling her, Jasmine didn't react fast enough, and the reins were wrenched from her hands.

Esme reared and bolted. Jasmine processed the sensation of sailing through the air a mere second before pain wracked her body, and the air was sucked painfully from her lungs. Her head slammed down and the bright, midday sun went black.

Seth ate lunch, though he didn't really taste the food. Carmen puttered around, but his focus wasn't on her, the plate in front of him or the list of things he was supposed to get done today.

It was hard to act normal, like nothing had changed in his life when in fact, nothing would ever be the same. How was he supposed to deal with that?

He'd known from the moment Zane had told him Jasmine was coming home that it marked a turning point. He'd felt it in his bones that things would irrevocably change as soon as she stepped back onto the ranch. He tried really hard to muster some anger at her for that, but he couldn't.

Somehow, somewhere, he'd let things spiral out of control. He had only himself to blame. As shocking as Jasmine's revelation was, he couldn't bring himself to be angry with her. She'd seemed too earnest and then too...devastated.

But he couldn't control or wish away the surge of jealousy that had overtaken him at the thought of sharing her with another man. He was only just now starting to come to terms with the fact that his feelings for her were forcing their way outward. He was having a hard time keeping them buried, locked away like some dirty, dark secret.

He hated himself for hurting her, something he couldn't seem to control, but he couldn't accept the sort of relationship she suggested. Could anyone? It had disaster written all over it. A prickle of irritation nipped at his neck. Why was he even giving the idea enough consideration to call it a disaster? He should be dismissing it as ludicrous, not weighing the potential hazards.

With a barely controlled sigh, he stood and took his plate over to the sink. When he glanced out of the window, he frowned.

Esme plodded inside the back fence, her reins dangling. Jasmine's camera case was still attached to the pommel and slapped at Esme's side as she wandered through.

"Carmen," he called. "Didn't you say Jasmine was taking Esme out for a ride?"

He heard Carmen shuffle back into the kitchen. "Yes. She left a note."

Seth swore and raced out of the kitchen, ignoring Carmen's startled questions.

"Jasmine!" he yelled as he exited the back door. He strode over to Esme and collected the reins. She was jumpy and skittish as if she'd endured a fright. Not taking the time to make sure she was properly put up, he yelled again for Jasmine.

His heart raced with panic. Jasmine wouldn't have let Esme wander around like that. Which could only mean that rider and horse had parted ways unintentionally.

He took several steadying breaths while he tried to process his options. He yanked his cell phone out of his pocket even as he ran for the shed that housed the four wheelers. Knowing Jasmine, she wouldn't have stuck to the roads, and he'd need the ATV to find her.

He punched in J.T.'s number as he straddled the four wheeler.

"J.T.," he said, not waiting for the other man to respond. "Jasmine's missing. She might be hurt. I could use your help down at the ranch. Esme came in alone. I think she may have thrown Jasmine. Zane's in San Antonio so I'm here by myself."

"I'll be right out," J.T. said grimly.

Seth hung up and fired up the ATV before roaring out of the shed and through the back gate. He crisscrossed the acreage, his eyes keenly attuned to every hill and scrape.

The sun beat mercilessly down and the hot wind blew over his face as he pressed the ATV to its limits. But he saw no sign of Jasmine.

An hour later, he paused to call J.T. to see where he was. He and another deputy were searching the eastern quadrant in places Jasmine might have ridden Esme. So far they'd come up as empty as he had.

He started off again, frustration beating incessantly at his temples. This was no place to get thrown from a horse. She could die of heat exhaustion in just a few hours' time.

He topped another hill and stared out across the creek that cut across the terrain. He was about to drive down into the bed when his gaze caught a flash of color a quarter of a mile away.

He gunned the engine and tore off at a breakneck pace. As he neared, he could see it was Jasmine lying on the ground. Sickening fear gripped him as he saw she was unmoving, her eyes closed.

He jumped off the four wheeler and ran to her. He sank to his knees and gently touched her face. "Jasmine. Jasmine, honey, can you hear me?"

Her eyelids fluttered open, and she smiled crookedly at him around cracked, dry lips. "I knew you'd come." Her face was pink from too much sun, and her green eyes were dull with pain. Dirt and grime accumulated in her hair and streaked her cheeks.

He reached out to touch her, wanting reassurance that she was okay. He closed his eyes as relief poured over him like cool, sweet spring water. "God, baby, you scared the shit out of me," he said hoarsely. "Are you all right? What happened and where do you hurt?"

"I tried to make it back," she said in a strained voice. "But my head and my ankle hurt like hell, so I laid down as much out of the sun as I could and waited for you."

That kind of faith humbled him and terrified him all at one time. "Did Esme throw you?"

"My fault," she mumbled. "Wasn't paying attention."

He gently gathered her in his arms and slowly got to his feet. He cursed when she winced against him. "I'm sorry, honey. I didn't mean to hurt you."

171

She shook her head against him. "I'm fine. Really. I didn't mean to make you worry. Was my own stupid fault."

He eased onto the four wheeler and cradled her against his chest. He was going to have to be damn careful driving back and carrying her this way.

Before he started the engine, he shifted Jasmine in his arms and pulled out his phone to call J.T.

"I found her," he said when J.T. answered.

"Thank God. Is she okay? Do I need to have an ambulance waiting?"

Seth glanced down at Jasmine's closed eyes, her head nestled trustingly against his shoulder.

"No, I don't think she needs one."

"Okay. I'll meet you back at the house."

Seth slid the phone back into his pocket then tightened his grip on Jasmine as he keyed the ignition. He headed back to the ranch, a lot slower than he'd come. He tried to absorb each bump and jostle, and he cringed each time her fingers dug tighter into his side.

When they rode past the gate, Carmen ran from the house along with J.T. and his deputy. J.T. reached for Jasmine so Seth could get off without jarring her further.

"Are you sure she doesn't need an ambulance?" J.T. asked doubtfully as Seth reached for her again.

"I'm fine, J.T.," Jasmine said in a weary voice. "I swear all I need is a hot shower and something for my headache."

"I need to look at your ankle too," Seth said as he carried her toward the house.

Carmen walked in behind him, clucking and fussing like an overwrought mother hen. Seth carried Jasmine up the stairs to her bedroom just as he had after the pool incident. Only this time, for some reason, she felt stronger. Not as breakable and fragile. Strange since this time she'd actually sustained a physical injury. Maybe his perception of her was changing.

"I started your shower," Carmen said as she rushed from Jasmine's bathroom.

"I think I want a bath," Jasmine said slowly.

Carmen looked at her in surprise and then smiled. "I'll go start a bath then."

"Put me down, Seth," Jasmine said quietly. "I can get myself into the tub."

He eased her down to her feet, holding her shoulder as he backed away slightly. She stepped forward, and her knees buckled. She let out a gasp of pain as her foot took the brunt of her weight, and she wavered precariously.

Seth swore and hauled her back into his arms. When she opened her mouth, he cut her off. "Don't argue with me. I'll get you into and out of the tub."

He felt her sag against him in defeat, and he strode over to her bed to lay her down. He tried to approach undressing her in a distant, medical fashion, as if she was merely someone he was concerned about, but the minute he uncovered her creamy skin, all thoughts of distance fled.

He clenched his jaw and tried to think of something, anything other than her soft curves he was fast uncovering. He concentrated instead on her ankle and examining her for other injuries.

When he touched the swollen skin above her heel, she hissed in pain. Without thinking, he leaned down to kiss the area. "I'm sorry, honey. I don't think it's broken, but you're going to have a devil of a time walking on it for a day or two."

She sighed but said nothing. When he looked up, he saw her green eyes glittering as she looked at him. There was a swirl of delicate patterns. Confusion. Hurt. Need. He was well-acquainted with the need. He wished he could be what she needed. All she needed.

Where the hell had that come from anyway? He shook his head. In an attempt to get his head on straight, he stood and bent to pick her up, intent on getting her into the bathtub.

He was too abrupt in his movements, and a small whimper escaped. His gaze flew to her face to see the strain around her eyes. Her mouth was compressed tight as if she hadn't wanted him to hear her cry out.

"God, it seems I'm always apologizing for hurting you," he said in self-derision.

He walked into the bathroom to see the water still running into the large garden tub. He lowered her into the steaming water. Her small, pink-tipped breasts slowly disappeared from view. They bobbed a bit in the water, and the swell was still evident over the rise of the water. It was a torturous sight for him. He wanted to touch her, lean down and run his tongue over that tempting strip of pale flesh, draw the puckered nipple into his mouth.

"Are you okay with this?" he asked. She never took baths, and he wasn't sure that day she'd jumped in the pool had completely cured her of her fears.

She let out a moan that sounded like a mix of pleasure and pain as she rested her head against the back of the tub. "I'm okay. Enjoying it too much to panic."

He frowned as he saw a bruise already forming at her hairline. He reached up to touch it then traced a path back further into her hair and saw a bloody cut.

"You probably need stitches. I should have taken you straight to the hospital," he said in a near growl.

She opened her eyes and focused her stare on him. "Seth, I'm okay. Really. No blurred vision. No nausea. I only lost consciousness for a bit."

He swore again. "The fact that you lost consciousness at all is a damn good reason for you to be in the hospital. How do you know how long you were out? You never wear a damn watch, and I doubt you'd have noticed what time it was on your way off the horse." The sarcasm crept into his voice despite his desire not to upset her.

She smiled then winced at what the action cost her. "It wasn't long. I just got the breath knocked out of me. I didn't push myself too hard trying to get back. I don't want to go to the hospital. I'd rather stay here with you."

Her words balanced delicately between them. Stood as a barrier. He wanted her here with him as well, and that was a huge problem. He reached up to turn off the water and stood awkwardly.

"I'll be in your room. When you're done, holler. I'll come get you."

Without waiting for a response, he turned and got out as quickly as he could, not caring that he was running like a coward.

Chapter Twenty-Two

Jasmine closed her eyes again and sank lower into the tub. She would sigh, but it would hurt too damn much. She felt like one giant bruise, and she was so tired she could feel exhaustion beating at her, beating her down.

She wanted him to hold her again. She'd stay in the tub for a long while, until the water cooled, but she knew the longer she made him wait, the more likely it would be that he'd run as far away from her as he could. And no matter that she'd forced herself to once again confront her fears, she still felt uneasy in the water.

So she soaked a few more minutes and then called out to him. He appeared seconds later, his expression controlled. As he came to the edge of the tub, he frowned.

"Aren't you going to wash your hair and that cut?"

"I'm not sure I can," she replied honestly. It wasn't a blatant play for his attention. She wanted to be in his arms, but she wasn't playing flirty little games with him. She wasn't sure she could lift her arms, much less undertake the arduous task of washing her hair.

His expression softened as he knelt by the tub. "Turn around," he said. "Scoot up and lean back so I can wet your hair."

She hesitated for a fraction of a second before she did as he said. The water swirled and sucked at her body as she positioned herself so he could better reach her hair. She folded her knees to her chest and inched forward. She nearly moaned in pleasure when his warm hands folded over her shoulders and guided her back so that she was reclined in the water. She swallowed some of her nervousness as the water worked higher over her body.

He held her with one hand and pulled his other hand through her hair until all the strands were soaked. "Okay, sit up, baby."

He pushed gently until she was once again sitting upright. She heard the squeegee-like sound of him squirting shampoo into his hand, and then he dug his fingers into her scalp.

She let her eyes flutter shut and leaned back into his touch. He massaged and lathered, working the soap into her hair. With each rub, she relaxed more. She didn't even flinch when he carefully worked around her cut.

"Like that?"

"Mmm hmm."

It was over too soon and he began to rinse her hair. She let out a small sound of disappointment when he signaled he was finished.

"Stay where you are," he ordered when she started to lift herself out of the tub. He plunged his arms deeper into the water and curled them underneath her knees.

With seemingly no effort, he lifted her out of the water. It streamed down her body and pelted the floor. He paused only to wrap a towel around her body and then one around her hair before he carried her into the bedroom.

He set her on the bed and pulled the covers down. "You want a T-shirt?"

She should say yes and make it easier for him, but why should it be so easy for him when it was so hard for her? She shook her head.

"Let me look at that cut now that it's clean," he said before she could shed her towel and climb underneath the covers.

He reached for the towel covering her head and pulled it away. He rubbed the cloth over her hair, ruffling it in an effort to dry it as much as he could. After a bit, he tossed it aside and put his hand back to her head. She sat still while he thumbed a part in her hair so he could view the wound.

"Am I hurting you?" he asked.

"No," she whispered. Though it wasn't entirely true. She couldn't stand this stiffness between them. He alternated between hot and cold, soft and hard with her. As if he couldn't make up his mind whether to love her or despise her. She was tired of feeling like a coin flip.

"It doesn't look bad. I'd feel better if a doctor looked at it, but I think it'll be okay."

She nodded slowly. Then she looked up at him and wondered at the picture they made. Him standing above her on the bed. Her sitting with just a towel wrapped around her, her heart in her eyes.

As if drawn to the image in her head, he lowered his hand until he cupped her chin. His thumb rubbed across her cheek in a sensuous line. She stared unflinchingly at him, not caring if she was broadcasting her need. She wasn't ashamed.

His head moved closer. She inched hers higher. His hand slipped away. His lips were just inches from her.

He stood to his full height, and she slumped in disappointment. "You should rest," he said gruffly.

"I'm not tired." And it was true. The exhaustion that had permeated her every pore just moments earlier had now washed away. Every nerve was standing on end, her awareness of him a living, breathing thing. "Stay with me. Please?"

Rife indecision carved lines across his face. At his sides, his fingers curled back and forth into fists, betraying his unease. When had things gotten so unbearable between them?

Just when she was convinced he'd say no and beat a hasty retreat from her room, he let out a small sound of defeat and sat down on the bed next to her.

"I'll stay if you rest."

She allowed some of the tension to escape her, and almost immediately, the fatigue was back. She sagged against the bed like a deflated balloon. Seth caught her and eased her down, then he moved up behind her and gingerly laid his arm across her waist.

She scooted back against his warmth, seeking the comfort of his arms, his touch, the feel of being melded to his body. She twisted restlessly against him until his arm tightened around her, a clear command for her to stop.

Edginess surrounded her. She itched on the inside.

"Relax," he murmured in her ear.

His hand came up to stroke her hair. She smiled and allowed herself to settle. She loved it when he touched her hair.

After a few minutes, the dampness from the towel chased a chill up her arms. Her skin prickled and rose with bumps.

"You need to get out of this towel," he said, though he didn't sound happy about the fact.

Instead of waiting for his inevitable retreat, she simply rolled and shimmied until she was free of the towel. She threw it across the room and pulled the covers up over her. She slid her naked back against his chest once more, wanting to restore their earlier closeness.

"Jasmine…" he began.

She rolled over to face him, her fingers seeking his face. "Don't go," she whispered. "Please, don't go."

She lifted her chin and pushed in closer until their lips met. He stiffened, his resistance clear in his body language.

She wrapped her hand around the back of his neck, encouraging him closer, *needing* him closer. "Please." She was begging. She didn't care.

Emotion swelled in her throat. Don't let him push her away again. God, please, no.

"Jasmine, I can't—"

She kissed him again.

"Jasmine." His voice grew quieter, his objection fading.

She kissed him again, pulling him still closer.

"I need you," she whispered. "Show me, Seth. Show me how it can be."

"You're hurt. You need rest."

"I need *you*." She wrapped both arms around his neck and pulled him down on top of her. He came, sliding his body along hers. She spent no time rejoicing over her victory. She didn't want to give him any chance to think better of it.

"I never meant to hurt you," he said, the pain in his voice making her shiver.

"I know you didn't. I should have told you it was my first time."

"It will be better this time," he promised.

"I know it will."

He crushed her to him, his lips molding to hers. He tasted her, devoured her, explored her with alternating roughness and tenderness.

There was a wildness about him that was ever-present, something he couldn't control, a part as integral to him as breathing, and yet, at times, he tempered it. He would pull himself back, she could feel it, as he skated close to the edge, he'd retreat, his movements gentling.

His kisses became more tender as his body moved urgently against hers, a compelling contrast, two motions completely at odds.

She pulled at his shirt, wanting to feel his bare skin, wanting to wrap his heat around her. He paused long enough to help her, yanking his shirt off. Then he knelt up and unbuttoned his jeans. He stepped off the bed and kicked off the remainder of his clothes, and she pushed up on her elbow, watching him there in front of her, naked, glorious, strong.

He stood for a long moment, allowing her the luxury of staring at his lean body. Her gaze skirted up and down his taut abdomen then lower to the juncture of his thighs. His cock, stiff, distended, jutted from the dark smattering of hair.

Hard, he was hard everywhere. Muscular, tight. His blue eyes blazed with lust as he looked down at her.

She opened her arms to him, inviting him back down, praying with all she had that he wouldn't refuse her. He lowered himself to her body, and she wrapped herself around him, her relief so strong it left her weak.

He kissed her neck, nipped and nibbled then soothed with his tongue. They were blanketed by their passion, their hunger for one another all-consuming.

For Jasmine it was all she'd ever wanted. For Seth? She could imagine it was all he ever wanted to avoid. The idea should hurt her, should drive the wedge of despair even deeper, but she clung to the small hope that he loved her but was too proud, too stubborn to give in.

She arched her neck, wanting more of his mouth, eager to feel his tongue on her skin. He skimmed along the hollow of her throat, lower to her chest and finally to the mounds of her breasts.

A sound of pure feminine appreciation escaped as he mouthed one nipple, licked over the tip then sucked gently on the bud. His fingers trailed down her sides, to her hips then feathered over her belly. He plucked at her belly ring before allowing his mouth to slide down to the dainty piece of jewelry at her navel.

"You did this for me," he murmured.

She smiled. "I did it because I knew it would drive you insane."

"Evil little wench."

She shifted restlessly underneath him, opening her legs, spreading them wider to accommodate him. He smiled at her blatant invitation.

"Kiss me...there," she said. "I want your tongue, your lips."

He nuzzled between her tender flesh and licked at the slick skin. Each swipe sent warm flushes streaking through her abdomen. Her body felt too warm, too flushed, too out of control. Her senses were not her own. They belonged to the man lying between her legs, his mouth taking her to her absolute limits.

He sucked lightly at her clit, not too hard, oh she loved that. Too hard would have been uncomfortable, but he seemed to understand the right balance between just enough pressure and not too much.

His tongue licked and flitted over each little sweet spot, her body tightening more and more with each stroke. Higher and higher she climbed, even as her mind protested. Not yet. She didn't want to come yet.

She didn't even realize that the whimper was hers. That the small uttered "no" spilled from her lips.

Seth raised his head, his expression intense, his eyes glittering with a dangerous need. She trembled when his hands gripped her thighs, and he slowly spread her legs wider.

He eased upward, his body moving along hers. Every scrape of his skin against hers sent a purr of contentment soaring through her throat. His hair-roughened legs slid along the inside of her thighs as he inched closer to her aching pussy.

Her hands met his face, cupped it, then she raised her lips to his. She wrapped her legs around his waist, and dragged her heels over his tight ass. Her ankle protested but she didn't care. The pain was nothing next to wanting to wrap herself around him as tight as she could go.

"How you tempt me," he whispered in seeming agony. "You're so beautiful. So innocent looking. An angel."

"Take me," she said. "Make me yours. Please."

The head of his cock rimmed her entrance, stretching it as he slid inside the barest of inches. Heat enveloped her like a brand. Her body stretched to accommodate him as he pressed forward.

"Tell me...if I hurt you," he gritted out.

She shook her head. "You're not."

With a small groan, he buried his face in her neck and surged against her, burying himself deep. A deep sigh of utter contentment rolled over her body.

He cradled her close, holding her, kissing her as he moved his hips against her. She dug her fingers into his back, wanting him closer, trying to absorb him into her soul. She never wanted this moment to end. Didn't want reality to intrude. Not now. Not ever.

He kissed her neck then slid his mouth up to her ear. His tongue circled the shell, sending shivers down her spine. Then he kissed his way down her jaw until he finally captured her mouth.

Soft then hard, breathless then slow. His lips moved over hers, sucking, tasting, taking and giving. She knew he was holding back and was conflicted by the desire to have him, hard, fast the way she knew he wanted and the warm, cherished feeling his tenderness gave her.

She closed her eyes and melted into him, giving him everything, all of her, holding back nothing even as he did.

"I love you."

The words fell from her lips, soft, from an aching throat, throbbing from tears unshed.

He tensed around her. He paused and held her long, tight. His body shuddered against her. She could feel his inner turmoil. His very real fight.

Then he began thrusting, deep, intense. He seemed to curl around every inch of her. Her pussy throbbed as her senses came alive, tightened unbearably as her orgasm mounted.

He slid his hands underneath her ass, cupping her cheeks with his big hands. He cradled her, holding her open to his invasion. Such a sweet invasion.

She moved her legs higher. Clutched him with her hands. Her eyes closed, opened and closed again.

"Don't stop. Please," she gasped as the room blurred around her.

"No, sugar, I won't."

She clenched her teeth together then sucked her lip between them in an effort to staunch her cry. Her body arched almost painfully into him and then something within her popped, setting her free.

She flew. Knew what it was like to have wings in that precious moment. When she reached as high as she could fly, her body fell back to earth, floating, spiraling downward in a gentle cessation.

"I love you," she whispered again.

Her eyes fluttered, and she dimly registered him closing around her, his body weighing on hers, his faint but steady heartbeat against her ribcage. He said something, but she was too far gone to hear what it was.

Chapter Twenty-Three

Seth stared down at Jasmine's sleeping form with a mixture of tenderness, self-loathing and ultimate satisfaction. He felt pulled in twenty different directions, none of which would get him anywhere.

He shouldn't be here, but the selfish part of him didn't give a shit. He wanted her. More than he should, but there it was. His guilt wasn't going to change that fact. Even as he knew he needed to get out of her bed, he leaned down to brush his lips across her temple.

She sighed softly and stirred as he brushed away tendrils of her hair. He stroked her soft skin and traced tiny paths in her hair.

Warm, soft, oh-so-feminine. She was in a word, perfect. But she wasn't his, would never be solely his, and he knew deep down that he couldn't accept that, could he?

Carefully, so as not to wake her, he eased away from her. He got up and walked around the bed to retrieve his clothing. His gaze was fixed on her as he pulled on his jeans.

She looked so young and innocent curled up in sleep. Her dark hair framed a delicate face. Her sweet curves beckoned to him. He was tempted to crawl back into bed with her and cradle her close, mold her softness to his and enjoy the feel of her against his skin.

186

But he didn't belong there. Zane did.

He winced as he thought of his brother and of the betrayal he'd just handed him. If Zane loved her, and he was obviously sleeping with her, Seth should never have gone back down that path. But he hadn't thought past his own burning need to make Jasmine his, if only for a short time.

His chest heavy, he turned and walked out of Jasmine's bedroom. When he hit the bottom of the stairs, he was met by Carmen. Her brow was creased with concern, and her eyes were questioning.

"How is Jasmine?" she asked, her accent heavier than normal.

"She's sleeping," Seth said. "You should go up and check on her in a little while. Wake her periodically. I don't know how hard she hit her head."

Carmen nodded. "And you, Seth? Are you okay as well?"

He cleared his throat uncomfortably. She wasn't stupid. She knew what was going on. "I'm fine, Carmen."

Her gaze softened, and she reached forward to enfold him in a hug. "All will be well. You'll see. You must follow your heart, eh? It knows the way of things."

He pulled away and smiled half-heartedly. "I'll be in the study if Jasmine needs anything."

Carmen nodded and headed up the stairs, no doubt to check in on Jasmine now. She was very much Carmen's baby. Seth trudged into the study and flipped on the light.

As he walked to the desk, he noticed several sheets of paper lying in the tray of the fax machine. He frowned. He didn't remember expecting a fax from anyone.

He picked up the pages and sat down behind the desk. As he flipped through them, his frown deepened. It was a contract.

An agreement for Jasmine to sign giving *Wildscapes* rights to print her photos. Why hadn't he heard anything of this? He would have thought she'd be excited. She damn near didn't go anywhere without that camera.

When he read the last page, a letter to Jasmine, he stiffened. It was a request for her to reconsider taking a position that apparently she'd already turned down.

He let the papers drop to the desk as he stared at the opposing wall. Why had she turned down her dream job offer? Even as he asked the question, he knew.

He folded his hands behind his head and leaned back, turning his head upwards, his gaze fixed on the ceiling above. His thoughts filtered to the conversation he and Zane had several days ago. About Jasmine's past. Her family. All that had happened to her six years ago.

He'd never once considered when he'd taken her home to Sweetwater Ranch, that she'd left behind any family, or at least someone she belonged with. Had he done her any favors by sheltering her so vigorously for all these years?

He'd been very approving when she wanted to move to Paris. It had been important to him that she spread her wings, experience the world outside the isolated West Texas ranch she'd lived on since she was sixteen. Deep down, he'd hoped she'd find happiness away from Sweetwater, even though he'd miss every part of her.

Had he and Zane made a mistake by never delving into her past? Was there someone out there wondering where she was? If she was alive? Zane mentioned a brother. If their sister was out there somewhere in the world, he'd damn sure want to know. But where was this brother when Jasmine had needed him most? What kind of man allowed his sister to fall prey to the worst sort of predator?

He heard a door close in the distance, and he stood and walked out of the study to see if it was Zane. It was, and he called out as Zane headed for the stairs.

Zane turned and looked inquiringly at him.

"How did it go in San Antonio?" Seth asked.

Zane put his foot down from the step and ambled over to where Seth stood. "Good. Got two bookings and several maybes. They were impressed by my presentation. Could be a good year for us."

"That's great," Seth said, though he knew his voice lacked enthusiasm.

"Is everything okay?" Zane asked sharply.

"Jasmine was hurt today. Esme threw her."

Zane's eyes widened. "Is she all right? Why didn't you call me?"

"Because by the time I found her, there was nothing you could have done anyway."

"Found her?" Zane asked in a strangled voice. "Was she missing?"

Seth rubbed a hand over the back of his neck. "Esme came back without Jasmine. I called J.T., and he and one of his deputies came out to help me look. I found her out about a mile. Got a knock to her head and a bum ankle."

"You didn't take her to the hospital?"

Seth made a face. "You know how stubborn she is. She just wanted to come home." It was on the tip of his tongue to tell Zane what happened, but he couldn't. He didn't want to see how his brother would react. Maybe he wouldn't care. Maybe he would. Seth didn't have any desire to find out.

"Where is she?" Zane demanded.

"Upstairs asleep."

Zane turned and without a word headed toward the stairs. Seth watched him go, his hands tense. He knew Zane would go up, touch her, make sure she was okay. Probably get into bed and hold her. Something she'd asked Seth to do earlier. He closed his eyes and turned away, unable to stand the thought of Jasmine in his brother's arms.

Chapter Twenty-Four

As soon as Jasmine became aware of the hard body wrapped around her, she knew it wasn't Seth. Her eyes fluttered open to see Zane staring down at her, his blue eyes filled with concern.

At what point had Seth left and Zane arrived? Instead of being put off, she drew such comfort from knowing that both had stayed with her. Both taking care of her, loving her, just as in her dreams, her most wonderful fantasies.

For a minute, she didn't say anything. She merely burrowed into Zane's strong arms, content to live in the moment.

"Are you okay, Jaz? Seth said you hurt your head and your ankle."

She pulled away. "What time is it?" she mumbled.

"Eight."

"In the evening?"

"In the morning," Zane said. "You slept all night."

Her brow furrowed. She vaguely remembered Carmen waking her at two different intervals. She'd grumbled but Carmen had insisted that she wake and answer questions. She'd complied then immediately fallen back asleep.

"Jaz," he prompted. "How are you feeling?"

"I'm good," she said. She stretched and flexed her ankle experimentally. Pain shot up her leg, and she couldn't control the grimace.

Zane latched onto it like a pit bull, yanking the covers down. He took her foot in his hands and brushed his fingertips across the swollen skin.

"You need to stay off this," he said grimly.

She sighed.

"Now show me where you hit your head."

She sighed again.

"Jaz," he said pointedly.

She lowered her head and pointed to the spot that ached. He burrowed his fingers gently into her hair, parting it so he could see the wound.

"Ouch," he said sympathetically. "Why the hell didn't you let Seth take you to the hospital? You probably need stitches. That's a hell of a gash."

She put her hand to his and pulled it away from her head. "I'm fine, Zane. Really. I've told Seth that until I'm blue in the face. I'm sure I'll walk around like an old woman for a day or two, but I'll be just fine."

"You shouldn't have been out riding Esme alone," Zane grumbled.

She arched an eyebrow and smiled at his concern. He certainly never used to mind her hell-raising ways. Heck, she'd taken off by herself more times than she could count. Half the time, she'd wound up at Tucker's only to be hauled out by J.T. But now Zane looked at her like a woman. His woman. It gave her a ridiculous thrill for him to be so worried and protective.

She put a hand on his cheek and coaxed him down so she could kiss him. "I love you. I missed you."

"I should have been here with you."

"Seth took care of me."

She sucked in her breath as the words fell. She hadn't meant to say it, even though she'd never made an effort to hide anything from Zane. But she didn't want to do anything that could potentially hurt him.

Zane seemed to read her worry. He kissed her tenderly, his lips melting over hers. "I'm glad he did, baby."

She sagged in relief.

"Now would you prefer breakfast in bed or do you want me to carry you downstairs so Carmen can fuss over you in the kitchen?"

She grimaced at the idea of spending the day in bed. "How about you leave me to take a shower and then I'll join you downstairs."

He gave her a doubtful look, but she shoved at his shoulders. "Go on. I can make it."

"Okay, but if you need help, holler."

She nodded. "I will. Now go. I'll be down in a few minutes."

He left her and disappeared out the door.

Jasmine scooted to the edge of the bed and swung her feet over the side. She tested her ankle, gingerly standing on her good one and then slowly putting her hurt foot on the floor.

Her knees nearly buckled when she put all her weight down. Pain shot up her leg and she wavered precariously. Damn, maybe she should have let him carry her.

With a barely suppressed grimace, she hobbled toward the bathroom determined to take a long, hot shower to remove the stove-up feeling in her body.

Fifteen minutes later, she stood at the top of the stairs. She wasn't sure exactly why she wouldn't let Zane take her down, but she didn't want to flaunt her relationship with him to Seth, even though Seth was well aware of her feelings for him. There was no sense waving the red flag in front of the bull.

She gripped the railing and stepped down with her good foot. Three steps later, she put too much weight on her sprained ankle and let out a cry of pain. Not a second later, Seth appeared at the bottom of the stairs and stared up at her.

He sprinted up, taking them two at a time. "Jasmine, what the hell are you trying to do? Fall down the stairs and kill yourself? Why in God's name didn't you call for me or Zane to carry you down?"

He didn't wait for a reply. He probably didn't want one anyway. He scooped her up in his arms, and she made a grab for his neck as he made his way carefully back down the steps.

They ran into Zane as Seth carried her into the living room. Zane took one look at her and bit out a curse.

"Hard-headed heifer. Didn't I tell you to call for me?"

"Uh, well, Seth sort of found me," she said.

"Going down the stairs," Seth said, scowling at her.

He set her down on the couch, and she stared up at him and Zane. She was getting a glimpse of how it would be with them. Both fussing over her, loving her, taking care of her. It created a powerful yearning deep within her. God, how she wanted both of them. Loved them. Needed them so much.

Zane got a pillow and propped her foot up on the coffee table with it while Seth positioned cushions behind her back. Emotion knotted in her throat until she thought she was going to break down and blubber in front of them both.

"Does your head hurt?" Seth asked in a low voice. "Do you want me to get you something for it?"

"Some ibuprofen would be great," she said, trying to control her shaky voice.

"Carmen is fixing breakfast now," Zane interjected. "I'll bring you a tray. We can all eat out here to keep you company."

Seth looked discomfited by the suggestion, and he turned and walked rapidly toward the kitchen. She met Zane's gaze, and for a moment they both stared. She had the strangest feeling that Zane was united with her in her effort to win Seth over. She didn't dare hope for it, and yet the idea gave her spirits a huge lift.

Zane smiled at her, his blue eyes softening as if he could see right into her darkest fears and biggest dreams.

"I'll go help Seth get the food. I'll be right back."

She watched him go, so afraid to believe. Despite her best effort not to nurture that hope, a small kernel unfolded within her. If only... If only they could both love her. It seemed so much to ask and so little all at the same time.

As they returned, trays in hand, she relaxed, determined to enjoy the morning with them both. It was almost like old times. But now when she looked at them, she did so with the knowledge of a woman, of the passion they could and had given her.

As content as she was with their lovemaking, the wild, insatiable part of her wanted to have them together. Their mouths on her body, their hands. Touching her, loving her, together and separately.

She nearly moaned aloud as the image burned brightly in her mind. Seth between her legs, Zane in her mouth. Zane behind her, thrusting into her. Seth in front of her, sliding into her mouth, his hands in her hair. One with his mouth on her pussy, the other's lips around her nipples.

She squirmed and closed her eyes, trying to shut out the barrage of arousal flooding her senses.

They ate and though Seth was largely silent, it wasn't as awkward as Jasmine feared. At one point, Zane reached over and slid his hand over her knee and up her leg. Seth's eyes tracked Zane's movements, and then he looked away as if unable to bear the sight.

Jasmine ached for him. For her. For all of them. She didn't want this to hurt. Love shouldn't hurt, though it did all too often. She wanted to make them happy. Both of them.

With an unhappy sigh, she pushed away her food, only half-eaten.

Seth stood and seemed all too content to take her tray and retreat to the kitchen. Jasmine leaned back against the cushions and closed her eyes. The medicine she'd taken still hadn't kicked in, and now her headache had worsened. The dull ache had blossomed into a sharp pain in her temples.

"Let me take you back to bed," Zane said softly. "You shouldn't be up."

She nodded, having no desire to argue the point. She did feel exhausted, and her earlier distaste for spending the day in bed vanished as the idea suddenly held a lot more merit.

She curled her arms around his neck as he picked her up from the couch. As he made his way to the stairs, she buried her face in his neck, absorbing his smell, the feel of him, his strength.

He rubbed his cheek over the top of her head in a comforting gesture as he walked up the stairs to her room.

He deposited her on the bed, tucked her underneath the covers and then kissed her lightly on the forehead. "You rest, Jaz. I'll come check on you later."

He'd always been so adept at reading her, and he'd obviously sensed her desire to be alone for a while.

"I love you," she managed around the tightness in her throat.

"I love you too, baby. Now get some rest."

Chapter Twenty-Five

After two days of being an invalid, Jasmine was ready to crawl out of her skin. Zane and Seth both fussed over her, but Seth seemed more distant with each passing day.

Her head no longer ached quite so vilely, and her ankle, while a little stiff, was no longer as swollen and so tender. She could manage quite nicely on her own, though she'd be lying through her teeth if she denied loving Zane and Seth carrying her around.

She stretched in her bedroom, flexed her ankle and walked around the room in circles. It was something she'd done each morning before one of the guys walked up to carry her down. This morning, though, she knew there was no point in leaning on them any longer. Her ankle was fine.

She stopped her pacing to stare out the window at the clouds rolling in from the southwest. They were in for a thunderstorm. It was a perfect day to stay in and listen to the thunder clap and the rain patter. She hoped it set in and wasn't just a quick shower.

After glancing at her watch, she grimaced. She'd napped way late. In another hour or two, Carmen would have dinner ready. If she went down now, she'd avoid being carried down later, and she could also sit and visit with Carmen in the kitchen and hopefully watch it rain.

After showering and dressing, she headed for the stairs, pleased when she navigated them without so much as a twinge. The living room was quiet and empty and Carmen hadn't taken up residence in the kitchen yet.

She'd take the opportunity to catch up on email and see if *Wildscapes* had faxed her contract to her yet. She'd almost forgotten about it with everything else that had gone on.

When she neared the study, she saw the door was open two inches, and she heard the murmur of conversation from within. She was about to push open the door and sing out a hello to Zane and Seth when she stopped cold.

She put her ear closer to the door, not sure she'd heard correctly. Were they talking about her family? Surely not.

"I think we've done her a disservice by shielding her all these years," Seth said. "We should have tried to locate her brother from the beginning."

"Maybe so, but I don't regret keeping her here," Zane said.

"I've made enquiries about him," Seth continued. "We owe it to Jasmine to make sure she has options." She heard the rustle of paper and then Seth resumed. "She turned down a position with a magazine. They wanted to hire her to do a regular column. She didn't even tell us about it. What else is she giving up because she thinks she wants to be here with us? I thought the year in Paris would do her good, but now I'm not so sure."

"Are you bringing him here?" Zane asked.

"She needs her own family," Seth said quietly. "We need to consider the possibility that she'll be better off with them."

Jasmine stepped away from the door, shock numbing her. His painful words echoed in her head. Seth, Zane and Carmen *were* her family. This was her home. Not with some brother she barely remembered and who cared nothing for her.

He couldn't have said any louder or clearer that she no longer belonged here.

She stumbled away from their voices. She had to get out, get away before she succumbed to the urge to confront them. She wanted to barge in there, demand to know what right they had to make decisions for her, but more than that, how could they say that she didn't belong here, that they weren't her family?

This betrayal hurt more than Seth's rejection, more than his harsh words, because this wasn't some front he was putting on for her. It wasn't something designed to deceive her. It was said when she was nowhere around, said to Zane when there was no ulterior motive. No reason for him to say it if he didn't really mean it.

A chill chased down her spine, and she shivered and rubbed her arms with her hands. She headed blindly out the back door into the warmth of the late afternoon. She walked, had no clear idea of where she was going. Panic clawed at her throat. She'd never considered that she wouldn't be welcome here.

In the distance thunder rumbled, and she remembered too late that a storm was due. When the first drops of rain splashed onto her bare shoulders, she looked up to see, to her surprise, that she was a good half mile down the road leading away from the ranch into town.

And now that she'd realized how far she'd walked, her brain caught up with her body, and her ankle whined its protest.

Still, she didn't turn back. The exercise would do her good. She couldn't go back until she knew what she would say. She couldn't pretend she hadn't heard. She trudged further down the road.

A few miles from the ranch and fewer still to town, the sky above her opened up and the rain fell in huge drops.

Yeah, the day couldn't get much better. She limped along like a bedraggled cat, hair plastered to her face, clothes stuck to her skin like a Seal-a-Meal bag.

She heard a rumble down the road and glanced up to see a truck headed her way. As it drew closer, she blew out her breath in a sigh. J.T.

He nearly zoomed by her, and then she heard the squeal of tires as he braked, nearly fishtailing into the ditch. She continued walking.

"Jasmine," he shouted behind her.

She walked faster.

He caught up to her and grabbed her arm.

"Jasmine, honey, what on earth are you doing out here in the rain for God's sake? You shouldn't be on your feet, much less three miles from the ranch. Where do you think you're going?"

"Away," she said dully.

His expression softened. Rain sluiced down his face, and he wiped the water from his eyes. "Get in the truck okay? In case you haven't noticed, it's damn wet out here."

"I'm not going back there," she said in a quiet voice. She shivered as more of the cold seeped into her skin. His hand tightened around her shoulder.

"You can go back to my place and get dry," he said.

She hesitated.

"Jasmine, I'm not leaving you out here on the road, in the rain. Forget it. Now get in."

She shrugged and allowed him to lead her back to his truck. He all but picked her up and shoved her into the passenger seat before walking around to get in on his side.

He executed a U-turn in the middle of the road and headed back toward town. He drove for a while in silence, and she stared straight ahead, watching the up-and-down swipe of his windshield wipers.

"What happened, Jasmine?" he finally asked.

Bitterness welled in her throat, and she looked out her window to avoid his gaze.

J.T. sighed. "What did Seth do now?"

She turned to stare at him in surprise. "You seem so sure it's Seth."

He grinned. "I don't think anyone else has the power to hurt you like he does. Am I wrong?"

She sighed. "No, you're not wrong."

His lips turned down into an expression of sympathy. "Handcuffs not work?"

Her shoulders shook with an almost laugh. "They want me gone."

J.T. took his eyes off the road again. "Now I know that can't be right, honey."

She shrugged. Started to tell him all she'd heard but then decided it just wasn't worth it. She turned again to stare out her window.

Several minutes later, J.T. pulled up outside of his house one block off Barley's main street and just two blocks from the police station.

"Come on inside so you can get out of those wet clothes." J.T. met her at the front of his truck and wrapped an arm around her shoulders to help her inside. The air conditioned air hit her smack in the face, and she shivered as water dripped from her body.

"Let me get you a T-shirt and some sweats you can change into. I'll put your clothes in the dryer," he said as he directed her toward the bathroom. "You can take a hot shower to warm up. I'll leave the clothes by the door."

She nodded and closed the door behind her. When she saw herself in the mirror, she winced. Drowned cat didn't quite do justice to the image staring back at her.

While she was grateful that J.T. hadn't insisted on driving her right back to the ranch, she also wondered what the hell she was doing here. It wasn't like she could hide forever. But bless J.T. for giving her a little time and not crowding her.

As hurt as she was by the conversation she'd overheard, she knew that she'd go back, and she had a choice. She could pretend she hadn't heard it, or she could take the bull by the horns and confront Seth and Zane about it. But if she did that, she had to be prepared to hear some things she might not want to hear.

She stood underneath the shower spray for a long time, enjoying the hot water on her cold skin. About the time she began to wrinkle up like a prune, she got out and shut the water off.

After wrapping a towel around her body, she peeked out of the door to see that J.T. had, indeed, left clothes on the floor for her.

She collected them and stepped back into the bathroom to pull them on.

A few minutes later, fully clothed again, she walked out of the bathroom. As she neared the living room, she heard J.T. talking in a low voice. An eerie sense of déjà vu closed in around her as for the second time that day, she heard her name in someone else's conversation.

"Jasmine's here, man, so don't have a cow. I picked her up on the side of the road when I was on my way out to see you. She's pretty upset."

Jasmine held her breath. How typical of J.T. to call and rat her out. So much for any damn loyalty among friends.

"I'll make sure she stays here until you come to pick her up," J.T. promised.

"Like hell you will," she muttered.

She turned, no longer interested in his conversation. She yanked on her still-damp tennis shoes and let herself out the kitchen door.

At least the rain had let up.

She stalked off, ignoring the slight protests her ankle made. She wasn't prepared to face Seth and Zane, and J.T. damn well should have known that. But he had no loyalty to her. That much was obvious. Men sticking together and all that shit.

She kicked at a can on the road as she headed in the general vicinity of Tucker's. Not that she'd stop there. She had no money on her, and it was the first place they'd look for her.

She shoved her hands deep into her pockets and continued walking. She cut across the open field behind Tucker's. The grass squished beneath her feet as the ground soaked up the rain like a greedy lover.

It was only six miles between town and the ranch. Plenty of time to think.

Chapter Twenty-Six

Seth roared up to J.T.'s house and threw open his door. Zane got out on the other side and they both hurried to where J.T. stood on the front porch.

"What do you mean she's gone?" Seth demanded.

J.T. blew out an aggravated breath. "Just like I said on the phone, man. She must have heard me talking to you. I thought she was still in the shower. When I went to look for her, she was gone."

"Fuck," Zane muttered. "Where did you find her anyway? Seth didn't say a damn word on the way here."

"I found her a few miles from the ranch heading this way. On foot. I almost didn't see her. I could tell she was upset. When I asked her where she was going, all she said was away. When I told her to get into the truck, she said she wasn't going back. I offered to bring her here so she could dry off at least."

"What else?" Seth asked sharply. "What could possibly have upset her so much that she set off on foot in the damn rain when she hurt herself just two days ago? Jasmine isn't stupid."

J.T. leveled a stare at him. "I asked her what you'd done to upset her. She seemed surprised by my assumption it was you. I suggested that you were the only one with the power to hurt her so bad."

205

Seth flinched and looked away. “She must have overheard.”

Zane swore. “Damn it, Seth, I told you it was a stupid idea. What was she supposed to think if she only heard part of that conversation?”

“She’d think we didn’t want her here,” Seth said in a low voice.

“Exactly.”

Zane’s chest heaved and fury was etched into his face. “Goddamn it. I’m sick of doing things your way, Seth. Fuck that. I’m done. Maybe you don’t give a fuck how badly you hurt her in your attempt to push her away, but I do. She doesn’t deserve this from us.”

Seth felt the words to his gut, each one sucking more air from his lungs. “Let’s just find her,” he said quietly.

“She’s upset,” J.T. said.

“Gee, you think?” Zane asked derisively.

J.T. held up his hand. “All I was going to say, man, was to cut her some slack. Give her a little breathing room. As Seth said, she’s not stupid. She just needs time to think.”

“She wouldn’t if Seth weren’t so intent on driving her away,” Zane said with a fierce scowl.

“Let’s go,” Seth said. “We need to find her and get her back home.” He didn’t want to have it out with Zane. Not here. Not now. Not ever.

ꕤ

Jasmine rubbed her palms up and down her arms as she crossed the small courtyard by the pool and headed for the kitchen door. She was tired, bone-achingly so. Her ankle throbbed, and it had rained on her again on the way home.

Every light in the house was on, and the courtyard was cast in the glow from the dusk to dawn light. She trudged up to the kitchen door and paused. Her hand curled around the handle, and she took a deep breath.

The door opened soundlessly and she walked inside. Seth stood abruptly from the barstool he was perched on, and without a sound, he yanked up his cell phone and punched a number. He put the phone to his ear.

"Zane, she's home. She's fine."

He hung up and stared at Jasmine, his expression thunderous.

"Where the hell have you been?" he asked as he stalked over to her.

She didn't reply.

"You had us worried out of our minds. And Carmen. She's upstairs in tears. Is that any way to treat a woman who has been a mother to you?"

"A mother you'd take away from me," she said bitterly.

He looked startled.

She took a step forward and winced.

Seth cursed and swept her into his arms. He gripped her tightly as he strode toward the stairs. Every part of him was tense. There was no sense putting up a fight so she lay limply against him.

He paused outside Carmen's door. "Carmen," he shouted. "Jasmine's home. I'm taking her to her room. She's fine."

Carmen burst out of the door but paused when she caught Seth's scowl. Carefully she leaned forward, captured Jasmine's face in her hands and kissed her cheek. "Thank God you're safe, *niña.*"

"I'm sorry, *mamacita,*" she whispered back. "I never meant to worry you."

Carmen patted her cheek. "I know this, *niña.* You are a good girl. Now go, let Seth take care of you."

Jasmine looked sorrowfully at her as Seth started forward again, his abruptness with Carmen bordering on rude.

Once inside her bedroom, he put her down close to the wall. She stumbled back, and instead of steadying her, he pressed in close to her.

He ravaged her mouth, his lips working so hot, so intensely over hers. Her back met the hard surface of the wall, and she was trapped between it and Seth's body.

"You test every one of my limits," he rasped as his mouth worked down her jaw and to her neck. "I have no control when it comes to you."

"You don't want me here anymore," she said quietly.

He stopped, his lips pressed to the hollow of her neck. Then he slowly stood to his full height. His eyes looked haunted as he reached out to cup her cheek.

"I've always wanted you here, Jasmine."

"You said that I didn't belong here. That you...that Zane and Carmen weren't my family."

Seth let out an agonized groan. He cupped her face in both of his hands and lowered his head to hers. He kissed her long, gently, his lips tender against hers. He pulled away the barest of inches.

"I just want what's best for you, Jasmine. And sometimes...sometimes I worry that we've cheated you by sheltering you here for so long."

"What if it's what I want?" she whispered brokenly. "I don't want to leave here. I love you."

Seth pulled her closer until her face was buried in his chest. He laid his cheek on the top of her head and breathed in deep.

The door flew open, and Seth pushed her away almost guiltily. Jasmine turned to see Zane standing in the doorway, his expression relieved.

"Thank God, you're okay," he said.

Seth stiffened beside her and started to move away. "I'll leave you two alone," he said in a low voice.

"Don't go," she pleaded, knowing this was it. Do or die time.

He paused and looked at her with uncertainty written in his expression. "What are you asking, Jasmine?"

"Make love to me," she whispered. "Both of you. I need you both so much. You were wrong. This *is* where I belong. With you. Both of you."

There was calm acceptance on Zane's face. Seth's was a wreath of torture. He was torn, and she could see that despite his objections, despite all that he'd said, he wanted her. She moved forward, her intent to make it as easy on him as possible.

She melted into his arms. At first he didn't respond, but when she trembled and faltered on her bad ankle, he caught her against him.

"You don't know what you're asking me to do," he said hoarsely.

"I'm only asking you to love me," she said softly.

She reached up on tiptoe to brush her mouth across his. As he pulled her to him, she turned her head to look at Zane.

She pleaded silently for him to understand, to accept. All she could see was answering desire.

Seth slid his hands from her back to the front of her belly. He tugged impatiently at her damp shirt. Zane stepped behind her and took it from Seth, pulling it the rest of the way over her head.

While Seth began shoving the baggy pair of sweats that J.T. had loaned her down her legs, Zane nudged her hair to one side and pressed his lips to her neck.

Instead of having her step out of the sweats, Seth simply lifted her and carried her to the bed. He set her down, and she leaned up, wanting to touch him, undress him as he'd undressed her. This was her fantasy, damn it, and she wasn't going to lie back and let it be dictated by someone else.

Behind Seth, Zane was already shrugging out of his jeans. Her mouth watered when she saw his cock slide free of the confining denim.

She worked at Seth's button then slid the zipper down. He aided her by taking his shirt off as she worked his jeans down over his hips.

"Pull it out for me," she whispered. "I want to see you."

He hesitated only for a moment before sliding his hand into his underwear. He pushed down the material then lifted his cock, holding it in his palm just inches from her mouth.

She reached out to cup his sac. She splayed out her fingers and stroked upward, finding the thick vein on the underside of his dick. She leaned forward and swirled her tongue around the blunt crown.

He flinched and issued a small grunt. She fisted him, moving her hand up and down as she sucked him deeper into her mouth.

The bed dipped behind her, and soon, Zane's hands trailed down her back, down to cup the globes of her ass. He spread them and sent his fingers seeking into the wetness of her pussy.

She closed her eyes, urged Seth deeper and let out a small moan of pleasure as Zane's fingers found her sweet spot. She rose up the teeniest bit to give Zane better access. She gripped Seth's hips and continued to suck him.

"On your knees," Zane said huskily. "Higher, baby."

She complied and positioned herself higher on her knees as Seth backed away to give her room. As she reached for Seth's cock again, Zane spread her with his fingers and moved to straddle her

She moaned as both men slid into her body at the same time. Zane's fingers dug into her hips as Seth's wrapped into her hair. They moved in unison, both thrusting deep. Then they began an alternating rhythm where one withdrew as the other thrust forward.

Seth reached underneath to cup both her breasts as he sank to the back of her throat. His thumbs brushed repeatedly over her taut nipples as Zane reached around to finger her clit.

She was bombarded by electric sensations. They fit together like lost pieces of a puzzle. They completed her in a way she'd never dreamed.

"Turn around," Seth said hoarsely. "I want that sweet pussy."

Zane withdrew, and she rotated around. Seth grasped her hips and in one motion, buried himself deep. She braced herself on her knees and cried out as pleasure burned her veins.

Zane lay back and reached for her head. He pulled her down until he thrust into her mouth. The taste startled her. It was her.

"Fuck, that's sexy," Zane muttered. "Lick me, baby. Taste your pleasure."

She sucked up and down, listening to his sighs of contentment. The slap of Seth's thighs against her ass grew loud in the quiet room. Each thrust pushed her further against Zane.

Zane stroked her hair, pulling it away from her face as he watched his cock disappear into her mouth. He seemed fascinated with the sight.

Seth surged deeper and deeper, and she could feel her orgasm burning, tightening, climbing higher and higher. She didn't want to go yet. She wanted it to last. She tensed and put a hand back to make Seth stop. He chuckled and slammed into her, holding himself deep.

"Let go, baby," he said huskily. "I guarantee it won't be your only orgasm of the night."

She squeezed around his cock as he pulled away again. Zane reached for her nipple as she pushed her mouth down over his cock. She closed her eyes as tiny little firework shows began popping in her abdomen.

Seth began thrusting wildly against her, and she lost what vestige of control she had remaining. She cried out around Zane's cock as they both drove deep.

She splintered, slowly, then faster, the tension in her pussy cracking and exploding. Warmth shot through her belly, spread throughout her body in one endless flush.

She was on a course to crash land, and she didn't care. She free fell from a cliff with no safety net in sight. As the room shifted and tilted around her, she closed her eyes and sucked Zane deep.

For several long moments, she merely existed, feeling nothing but the most intense pleasure as both men rocked against her.

Finally her muscles went limp and she sagged. Seth caught her hips and eased his movements until he slid back and forth with exquisite tenderness.

Seth pulled her away from Zane and turned her with his hands. "Lay down, baby," he said huskily.

Zane got to his feet and reached for her shoulders, positioning her so her head hung over the edge. Seth crawled up onto the bed and eased between her legs.

"Just lay back and let us take care of you," Zane crooned.

His words were such a sweet balm. Words she'd waited forever to hear.

Zane rubbed the head of his cock over her lips, coaxing her to open for him. When she did, he slid deeper. His hands crept to her jaw, holding her as he gently fucked her mouth.

Seth ran his fingers over the seam of her pussy and parted the sensitive folds. She still quivered from her orgasm and each touch sent a jolt of almost painful sensation through her pelvis.

He reached underneath her to cup her ass, opening her further to him. Zane palmed her breasts and plucked lightly at her nipples, oh-so-sensitive from her orgasm. Seth pushed forward, planting himself deep inside her body.

They both rode her, at first with sensual decadence, their rhythm slow and restrained. But as their breathing grew sharper, their pace increased. Their thrusts became harder, their hands became more seeking.

Unbelievably, she felt the stirrings of another orgasm. Sweet, thrilling, delicious. Seth pulled her legs up, holding them high over his arms. He pumped against her as Zane filled her mouth over and over.

She squirmed underneath them and wondered how the hell they were holding out so long when she was well on her way to her second orgasm. And to think she'd been worried about it all being over in thirty seconds. If they wanted to give her multiple orgasms, who was she to complain?

"I'm going to come," Zane whispered. "Tell me if you want me to pull out."

She shook her head vigorously and sucked him deeper. She wanted all of him. Wanted to taste him, wanted to give him the same satisfaction she'd found.

His fingers tightened at her breasts and then they flew to her face. He held her tightly and let out a sexy groan. Hot fluid spurted against the back of her throat. It filled her mouth, and she swallowed rapidly as more splashed against her tongue.

He thrust deep as the last of his orgasm danced in her mouth. He held himself there for a long moment as his hips jerked and quivered. Then he pulled away, and she licked the thin trickle of fluid from her lips.

Zane immediately moved to the bed and bent his dark head to her breasts. His hair brushed the tips as he positioned himself so that he could access either nipple.

As Seth continued his erotic assault on her pussy, Zane sucked one nipple deeply into his mouth. She arched into him and cried out. His hand found her other nipple and he twisted it between his fingers.

"Oh God, I'm going to come again," she gasped out.

"Then come," Seth gritted out. "I'm close, baby. Come with me."

She didn't need any encouragement. As Seth pounded between her legs, her orgasm built sharply, much faster than her first. It was on her almost before she was aware that she was hurtling over the summit.

Seth called her name just as she felt him strain against her. A flood of warmth filled her, and still it came. She hovered, buzzing and burning. And then she went off like a sling shot.

Zane sucked lazily at her breasts, and she raised a weak arm so she could trail her hand through his hair. Such sweet contentment. Seth slowly eased from between her legs and crawled onto the bed beside her.

He lay down, propped on one elbow, and Zane pulled away from her nipple. Strong hands caressed and petted her skin, her tired muscles. Their touch was loving, tender. She arched and purred like a kitten.

"Want a bath?" Seth murmured.

Instead of instilling panic, the idea pleased her. She nodded and he leaned down to kiss her.

"I'll draw you some water, but don't take too long. I'm already hungry for you again."

She shivered at the promise in his voice. "Maybe I'll just take a quick shower."

She started to get up, and when she put weight on her ankle, she grimaced. She hadn't done it any favors by all the walking she'd done today.

Zane was there. He swept her up into his arms and started for the bathroom. To her surprise, Seth followed behind. Seth reached in to turn on the water and Zane stood back, still holding her tight in his arms as he waited for the water to grow warm.

Seth motioned for Zane to move forward but when he got to the shower, Seth reached for Jasmine. "I'll take her," he said in a low voice.

Zane set her down and kissed the top of her head before ambling back toward the bedroom.

Chapter Twenty-Seven

Seth stepped into the shower and pulled Jasmine in after him. His arms folded around her as the hot spray rained down on them. He nuzzled her neck as his hands slid down her body to cup her ass.

He seemed insatiable, like he couldn't get enough of her. As if he'd waited forever, like she'd waited for him.

Her legs trembled and her knees buckled. If he hadn't been holding her, she would be in a puddle in the bottom of the shower.

He soaped her body, paying special attention to her breasts and nipples. Then he ran his hands between her legs and gently washed the tender folds. A few minutes later, he nudged her from the shower and proceeded to dry her with a towel. Instead of wrapping the ends around her, he dropped it on the floor and stood back, looking at her naked body.

"You're so beautiful," he said hoarsely. "So young and wild. How can any man ever hope to keep you?"

Her brow furrowed at his words. She wanted to protest, to tell him she was his, but her effort was stifled when his lips crashed down on hers.

"You're mine," he said. "For tonight you're mine to take as I want."

"Yes," she whispered.

He cupped her face in his hands. "Go into the bedroom. Get on the bed. When I come in there, I want you to be sucking Zane's cock. Ass in the air. Waiting for me."

Her eyes widened but she nodded.

"You wanted to be between us, like the other women," he said. "It's time you found out just what that entailed."

She swallowed and nodded again.

"Go."

She turned and walked into the bedroom where Zane was lying on the bed. He was a beautiful sight to behold, all wild and bold, legs outstretched. His hand was on his cock, stroking, his eyes half-lidded.

She walked to the bed, mindful of Seth's instructions. She crawled between Zane's legs, letting her hair fall over his legs.

She watched for a moment, the slow up and down movement of Zane's hand as he gripped his cock tighter. His legs were thick and muscular, and they rippled as he arched his hips. His cock was surrounded by jet black hair, and his heavy sac tightened and loosened with each upward tug.

She lowered her head and ran her tongue up the length. He shuddered and let go with his hand so she could continue her upward path. When she reached the tip, she closed her mouth around it and sucked him deep.

His hands tangled in her hair, pulling her closer. She almost forgot Seth's second instruction as she lost herself in the taste and feel of Zane.

She spread her legs and arched her ass in the air.

"Good girl," Seth purred.

She turned her head, letting Zane's cock slide from her mouth. Seth stood beside the bed, his eyes burning with arousal. He reached out and trailed his hand over her back and then over the curve of her ass.

"Go back to what you were doing," Seth murmured.

She refocused on Zane and sucked his cock back into her mouth. Seth climbed behind her and grasped her hips in firm hands. He locked her to him, and his cock nudged impatiently at her entrance.

He thrust shallowly for a moment until she whimpered in protest. Giving in to her demand, he plunged forward, riding her hard and deep. Each forward motion pushed her harder into Zane, drove his cock deeper into her throat. She gloried in the taste of Zane and the feel of Seth, both connected to her, body and soul.

Zane lifted her head and stared down into her eyes. "Can you take us both, Jaz? Can you ride me while Seth rides you?"

A quiver started in her belly, fanned out and burst over her body like a ball of flames. She licked her lips and looked hungrily at him. Didn't he know that this was what she'd always wanted? To be loved and cherished by both of them? To show them both how much she loved them?

She was no naïve girl when it came to threesomes. Cherisse had filled her mind with erotic images. She'd fantasized about Seth and Zane taking her in just about every conceivable way.

Seth eased from her pussy and Zane reached for her, pulling her on top of him. He reached down and positioned his cock underneath her then pushed her down with his other.

She let out a gasp as he pierced her deeply. Zane groaned and grasped her hips in his big hands.

"Move with me, baby," he said as he turned so his legs fell over the edge of the bed. He held her tightly as he positioned himself.

Then she felt Seth's hands slide up her back to grasp her shoulders. He gathered her hair in his fingers and let it slide over his hands.

"Beautiful," he whispered.

He let his hands glide down her body until they reached her hips. Zane let go as Seth's hands replaced his. One hand left her, and she heard the unmistakable sound of liquid squeezing from a bottle.

One hand slid between her ass cheeks and spread. The other hand smoothed the cool lubricant over the sensitive opening. She jumped when he inserted one finger just inside the tight ring.

"Easy. I won't hurt you, sweetheart."

He shifted behind her, and then she felt the broad head of his cock press against her anus. Zane reached between their bodies to touch her clit. He fingered her softly while Seth eased forward.

She closed her eyes and leaned further into Zane. A soft moan escaped her at the unbearable tension unraveling her thread by thread.

And then he was inside in a sudden burst of relief. They both let out an agonized cry. Zane latched onto her nipple with his mouth as Seth slid all the way inside her ass.

Her head went back as they began an alternating rhythm, one withdrawing, one thrusting deep into her body. She yanked Zane's head away from her breast and slammed her lips down over his. She kissed him hungrily, tasting him, sucking his bottom lip between her lips.

His hands slid up her arms and gripped her shoulders, pulling her closer even as Seth slapped against her ass with increasing force.

She allowed the image of how they must look to float in her mind, arousing her to even greater heights. Sandwiched between two men she loved more than anything, giving herself wholly to them, never had she felt more complete. Never again would she find this kind of love.

She rose up, reaching over her head for Seth. She pulled him to her, meshed tight against her back. He ravaged her neck with his mouth, kissing and nipping at her skin. She turned her face to him, holding his head to her as the two men continued to thrust into her wanting body.

Whispered cries of ecstasy ripped from her lips. Seth pressed her down toward Zane, and she lay across his chest, completely surrounded by male flesh. Each thrust by Seth forced her further into Zane's arms. She closed her eyes and clung tightly to Zane as her orgasm began a slow climb.

"Are you close?" Seth asked in her ear.

"Y-yesss," she hissed. "Oh God, please don't stop."

Zane chuckled. "Never, baby."

She dug her fingers into Zane's shoulders as both men plunged deep and paused. Never had she felt so full. So stretched. So unbelievably pleasured.

Her mouth opened as a cry escaped. The room darkened and her head swam. Her orgasm flashed and exploded. She felt a twinge of disappointment that it had ended so quickly when unbelievably she felt the hard rush of another.

"Oh. Oh!" she said louder.

Warmth flooded her ass as Seth jerked against her. Zane surged upward, and a few seconds later, his head went back, his hands grabbed desperately at her hips as he spilled into her.

She twisted, panting, her orgasm so close. Seth pushed against her again and reached around to cup her breasts. He rolled her nipples between his fingers as Zane reached down to rub her clit.

A hoarse cry escaped in a painful rush. Her body convulsed, and she collapsed forward. Zane caught her and both men cradled her shaking body.

Seth pressed his lips to her shoulder and kissed a line to her neck. She felt Zane's breath, hot and unsteady in her other ear.

Slowly and with great care, Seth eased from her body.

"Sit tight, baby. I'll be right back."

Zane held her, stroking his hand up and down her back while she waited for Seth to return. A few moments later, Seth pressed a warm cloth to her behind and wiped gently. When he pulled away, Zane rolled her beneath him and pulled his still semi-hard cock from her quivering pussy.

He kissed her and flopped to his side, pulling her against his chest.

"I'm gonna grab a quick shower," Seth said.

She looked up and their gazes connected. He stared at her for a long moment before turning and heading toward the bathroom.

Zane's arms tightened around her and she snuggled closer into his embrace.

"You okay, baby?"

"Mmm hmm," she said, letting out a sound of pure contentment.

She lay there, drifting in a state of dreamlike euphoria. Then she felt the bed dip as Seth climbed in behind her. He seemed to hesitate for a moment before finally sliding a hand over her hip.

His lips found her ear and he kissed her. She shifted back, so that her body conformed to his. His heat surrounded her, warmed her to her deepest recesses.

Seth behind her. Zane in front. Nothing, absolutely nothing could be more right. If she could live in this moment forever, she would.

Chapter Twenty-Eight

Jasmine knew he was gone before she ever opened her eyes. Her chest caved a little, and achy emotion swelled in her throat. She was turned to Zane, burrowed into his chest, and his arms were wrapped around her, but where Seth had lain the night before, warm against her back, there was now a coldness that transcended the actual temperature.

"Morning," Zane said softly in her ear.

For some reason his gentle words knocked open the gate, and she let out her breath in a shaky sob.

Zane reached down and tugged her chin upward with his finger. He didn't say anything, but his expression made words unnecessary.

"Do I have a chance of ever making him love me?" she choked out.

Zane kissed her forehead. "He loves you already, sweetheart. And that's the problem. It's killing him."

She twined her arms around his neck and hugged him tightly, her naked body fitting to his. "I never wanted to hurt him, Zane. Either of you. I swear."

Zane ran his hand through her hair, stroking and soothing. "I know, Jaz. I know. He just needs...time." But Zane didn't sound convinced of that.

"Make love to me, Zane," she said against his neck.

And he did. Sweetly, hungrily. Many long moments later, they lay side by side. Exhaustion tugged at her every muscle, but still, she'd wanted, needed this reassurance after Seth's hasty departure.

Zane moved away as he made to get out of bed. He looked down at her, his expression serious. He touched the side of her cheek with gentle fingers. "Get some sleep, Jaz. You need the rest after yesterday. I'll be up later to check on you."

She nodded and turned her face into his palm, nuzzling against his touch. Her eyes were closed before he ever made it to the door.

Zane found Seth standing on the edge of the food plots, staring out into the distance. His stance was stiff, troubled. Zane didn't waste time on pleasantries or pretending he wasn't out here to talk to his brother.

He came to stand beside Seth and looked sideways at him.

"You're hurting her."

Seth turned his brooding stare on him. "Don't you think I know that?" He shook his head and returned his gaze to the land. "As much as it's hurting her, it's hurting me more. I don't know that I can share her with anyone. Not even you. I don't know if I can accept that I can't make her happy by myself. Provide and care for her alone."

Zane didn't say anything for a long moment. Seth's concerns weren't anything that hadn't crossed his own mind more than once.

"I understand," he finally said, because what else was there to say? Seth would have to make his own decision and in his own time.

"It's probably too late anyway," Seth mumbled. "She might hate me after tomorrow."

Dread niggled at Zane. "What have you done?"

Seth stuffed his hands in his pockets. "Her brother is arriving tomorrow."

Zane stiffened, an unknown fear skating down his spine. "What the fuck? Seth, you know how she feels about that. Why would you blindside her like that?"

Seth shook his head. "I wasn't thinking. I was reacting. And now it's too late. He knows she's here, and he wants to see her. You and I can't deny him that."

"It's not up to us to deny or allow him anything," Zane said bluntly. "It should have been Jaz's decision. Not yours."

"I know," Seth said quietly.

"Are you going to tell her?" Zane demanded.

"Tonight."

Zane looked away. Jaz would be upset. She'd see it as one more way Seth was trying to push her away and by association, he would be damned as well.

"I never tried to come between you and Jasmine," Seth said. "I knew she loved you, too. I won't lie and say I wasn't jealous, but I never tried..."

"I know," Zane said quietly.

"You don't mind that the woman you love is fucking another man?" Seth asked in a strangled voice.

Zane was silent for a time. This was too important. Too important to Jaz for him to get hot-headed and fuck it all up.

"It's not just another man," he finally said. "It's you. You love her as much as I do no matter that you might say differently. And she loves us both. How could I ask you to deny your feelings for her?"

He turned and walked back toward his truck. Seth being Seth would need to stew and brood. Zane was too worried about how Jaz would react when she found out her long-lost brother was coming to visit.

ℋ

Jasmine dressed slowly. Her body was still in a languid state from Seth and Zane making love to her. In truth, all she wanted was to go back to bed and hold those memories close. Both men loving her, touching her, filling her.

She trudged down the stairs and looked around for Carmen. For Seth or Zane. But it was quiet. In the kitchen, she found a note on the fridge from Carmen saying she'd gone grocery shopping and would be back later.

She rummaged around for a snack, but it was tasteless on her lips. She chased it down with water and walked over to the window to look out. Seth and Zane were nowhere to be seen. She set her glass down in the sink when she heard the front doorbell.

With a frown, she turned around to go answer the door. They didn't get many visitors out this way, though it could be J.T. dropping in. If Seth and Zane weren't around, he wouldn't just barge in the house.

She gripped the knob and swung it open, startled to see a man standing on the doorstep, an odd expression on his face. He was handsome, maybe around Seth's age. His hair was the same dark shade of brown, almost-black that hers was, and when she stared into his eyes, she saw her own looking back at her.

"Jasmine, my God, is it you?" he said in a strained voice.

227

He started forward, enfolding her stiff figure in his arms. She panicked and broke away, backing into the house as fast as she could go.

She bumped into Zane who wrapped a protective arm around her to steady her.

"Jaz, honey are you okay?"

"Who is he?" she stammered out, pointing toward the door.

Once he saw the man inside the door, he shoved Jasmine behind him.

"Who are you and what the hell are you doing in my house?" Zane demanded as he advanced menacingly.

"Zane, back off," Seth said in a quiet voice.

Jasmine turned to see Seth standing behind her, a strange look on his face. It almost looked like fear.

"It's her brother," Seth explained.

Jasmine returned her gaze to the man standing just a few feet away. Her mouth fell open as shock spilled over her. Then she turned back to Seth.

"How could you?" she whispered. "Did you want me gone so badly?" She wrenched away from Zane, who had reached out to take her hand. She ran for the stairs, uncaring of the pain in her ankle.

Seth watched her go in despair. There was no way she'd forgive him for this. If he lived to be a hundred, he'd never forget the look of absolute hurt in her eyes.

"I take it I haven't come at a good time," her brother said.

"You weren't supposed to be here until tomorrow," Seth said pointedly. "I hadn't gotten a chance to tell Jasmine about you yet."

The man sighed. "I'm sorry. It's just that I couldn't wait any longer to see her."

Brazen

Seth walked forward. "I'm Seth Morgan. This is my brother Zane."

Her brother reached out to shake his hand. "I'm Cody Quinn, Jasmine's brother."

"Where the hell have you been for the last six years?" Zane snarled. "Hell, longer than that. Where were you when she was eking an existence out on the streets, depending on survival from a man determined to sell her body to the first willing customer?"

Cody's face went ashen.

Seth held up a hand. "Not now, Zane. We need to hear what he has to say before we let him talk to Jasmine."

Zane pressed his lips together and looked away.

"Let's go into the living room," Seth suggested. "I very much want to hear what Cody has to say."

℘

Cody stood with his back to the two brothers, staring out the window a half hour later, after Seth had related how he and Zane had met Jasmine. "I never knew what had happened to her," he said.

"When I learned of Mom's death, I arranged leave and got back as fast as I could. They told me she was in a foster home. I went and talked to my CO and arranged for even more time away. I wanted to try and make a home for her. When I got back, though, she'd run away. I searched for her, did what I could. When I'd exhausted all my resources, I went back to work, but I continued looking. Over the years, it became easier to believe that I'd never see her again and the searches tapered off."

He turned back around to stare at Seth and Zane. "Until I got your phone call a few days ago, I wasn't sure if she was alive or dead."

Seth could see the sincerity in Cody's eyes. "I'll be honest. I'm not sure Jasmine will agree to see you."

Cody nodded. "I can understand. She probably feels as though I deserted her when she needed me most. But I'd like the chance to explain, at least to talk to her."

"I'll see what I can do. I can't make any promises."

Chapter Twenty-Nine

When Seth stepped into her room, he saw Jasmine standing in the window, staring out. He moved closer, and he could see the slight tremble of her body.

He slid his hands over her shoulders and down her arms.

"I'm sorry, Jasmine," he said simply. "I shouldn't have sprung this on you. I intended to tell you tonight."

She turned slowly, her eyes haunted, hurt reflected in her emerald gaze. "Why is he here?" she asked in a small voice. "Why now?"

Seth sighed and pulled her into his arms. "I think you should talk to him, honey. Hear what he has to say. He's very anxious to see you."

"You want me to go," she said dully.

He tightened his grip around her. The idea of her leaving panicked him. But it would be her choice. It wasn't his to make.

He pulled her away and tipped her chin up until she looked him in the eye. "I want what is best for you. I always have."

"You're what's best for me," she whispered. "You and Zane. And Carmen. We're family."

She slid away from him before he could respond. "Is he...is he still here?"

"He's downstairs waiting for you," he replied.

She nodded. "I suppose I should go down."

She looked toward the door and hesitated.

"Zane and I will be there, Jasmine. You won't be alone."

She nodded again and turned wordlessly to walk out. Seth followed her, concerned by the defeated slump of her shoulders. She was quiet on the way down the stairs, and when they reached the living room, she paused as if afraid to go in.

Zane looked up at the same time Cody did. Worry was reflected in both their gazes. Seth put his hand comfortingly on Jasmine's back.

Jasmine stood there, staring at her brother, her *brother*, with a mixture of elation, sadness and fear.

Memories of her childhood ran through her mind. Her as a little girl, Cody smiling down at her. Cody and her mother arguing as she got older. That last terrible night when Cody had left and sworn never to return.

He'd left her.

Cody stood and walked cautiously toward her. He stopped a few feet in front of her and slowly raised his arms, holding them out to her.

Swallowing back her fear, she walked into his embrace.

He hugged her tightly, stroking her hair. "My God, Jasmine, I can't believe it's you."

She didn't respond. She closed her eyes and absorbed his hug. After several minutes in which he merely held her, he gently pulled away.

"There's a lot I want to say to you, Jasmine. A lot we need to catch up on."

She nodded.

Seth cleared his throat. "Carmen should be back soon. Will you stay for dinner, Cody?"

"If Jasmine wants me to," he replied.

"I'd like that," she said softly.

"Why don't we get comfortable?" Zane suggested, making it clear he had no intention of leaving Jasmine alone with Cody.

Cody led her over to the couch, and she sank onto the cushions, grateful because she wasn't so sure her legs would support her anymore.

She licked her lips nervously and focused her gaze on her brother. He was big, muscled. His years in the military had obviously honed his body. He still wore his hair short, and she wondered if he was still enlisted.

The silence was awkward and so she said something, anything to alleviate the strain. "Tell me about you?"

The question seemed ludicrous. He was her brother, and yet, here they sat, two strangers.

He reached for her hand, but she stiffened, and he pulled away. She balled her fingers into fists and kept them in her lap. She wondered if he was insulted by her rebuff, but she couldn't bring herself to care.

"I'm married. I have a young son. He just turned one." His expression softened as he spoke of his family. Hurt welled in her throat. His family that didn't include her.

"Are you still in the military?" she croaked.

He shook his head. "Not for three years. I own my own construction company now."

"Where?"

"Just north of Baton Rouge."

"Not far from home then," she said faintly.

"No," he replied. "I never wanted to leave that area in case...in case you came back."

She turned her chin up and stared at him. "Why didn't you come back?"

Sadness and regret crowded his green eyes, eyes that were so much like hers. "I did, but it was too late. You'd already gone. I never should have cut myself off the way I did. I couldn't see past my anger with Mom. I never expected her to die. I assumed you'd be happy with her and her new husband."

"She never married him," she bit out.

He reached for her hand again and this time she didn't pull away. "Jasmine, I let you down. I'll never forgive myself for that. But you could have come to me, too."

Shock held her immobile. He was right, but he hadn't made her feel as though that was an option. Ever. "I didn't think you'd want me," she said simply. "You never called or wrote. It was as if you forgot all about me and Mama."

Cody looked away. When he looked back, regret shone in his eyes. "I'm sorry, Jasmine. Sorrier than I can ever say."

His hand tightened around hers. "My wife and I would like you to come stay with us. You'd have a home with us as long as you like."

Her eyes widened in shock. "But—" She broke off. Her protest died. Seth and Zane no longer wanted her here. They were the reason Cody was here. "I'll think about it," she finally said.

She spent the rest of the afternoon in light, careful conversation with Cody. He told her about his wife and their one-year-old baby. His business was successful, and his wife was a registered nurse who worked in a local hospital.

It was hard not to warm to him. He seemed sincere and cautious about overwhelming her too soon. Several times he seemed to want to hug her, but he backed away, giving her space. She invited him to stay the night since he hadn't stopped in town to get a hotel.

Dinner was quiet, and Carmen spent much of the time either chattering endlessly or looking like she'd burst into tears at a moment's provocation.

Jasmine picked at her food and finally buckled under the strain of the day's events.

"I'm going up to bed," she said quietly.

The men watched her as she stood and pushed her plate aside. Cody gave her a reassuring smile, and she attempted one in return. She avoided Zane's and Seth's gazes as she walked out of the kitchen.

Instead of going to her bedroom, she eased into Seth's room. She undressed and pulled on one of his old T-shirts, something that had brought her comfort in the past.

She crawled underneath the covers and curled her legs into her chest. Sleep would be difficult, though she felt exhausted and emotionally drained. She settled in to wait for Seth, her heart heavy and sad, afraid of what he would say.

Chapter Thirty

Seth walked into his bedroom, though he knew he wouldn't sleep. Too much was going on in his mind, and it was too late to stop the chain of events he'd started from unfolding.

He froze when he saw Jasmine curled up in his bed. His bed lamp was on, and he could see that she'd fallen into a troubled sleep. He stepped closer, surprised to find her here. In the past, she'd always gone to Zane for comfort, a fact that made him jealous though he never admitted as much. Until recently.

Her face was crinkled, her brows drawn together in tension. Her bottom lip was drawn between her teeth, and he could see red blotches on her cheeks from crying.

With an odd catch in his chest, he sat down on the edge of the bed and reached out to stroke her cheek. She stirred and opened her eyes to stare at him.

"Do you think you could ever love me?" she asked in an aching voice.

As complicated as it made things, he knew he couldn't lie to her. It would be easier, easier for all of them, if he just said no, that he didn't love her.

"I do love you, Jasmine. Maybe I always have."

"Then why don't you want me?" she whispered.

"I want you, Jasmine. That's the problem. I want all of you, and I can never have that. I can't...I can't accept having just a part."

Jasmine felt her heart crack and crumble around her. The quiet resolve in Seth's voice told her that he'd made up his mind.

"I'm sorry, Seth. I'm sorry to have caused trouble between you and Zane. That was never my intention. I left here a year ago because I couldn't resolve my feelings for both of you. While I was in Paris, someone opened my eyes to the possibility of a relationship that involved both of you. I took an exception and tried to make it the rule, and for that I'm sorry. I couldn't see beyond my own needs and desires. I had hoped...I had hoped that maybe you could both love me the same way I love the both of you."

She pushed herself into a sitting position and then eased off the bed, her heart breaking with every single movement. When she was standing, she turned back around to where Seth still sat on the bed, his eyes haunted.

She leaned down and brushed her lips across his, closing her eyes as she savored this last moment with him. "I love you. I will always love you."

She straightened back up and took in a steadying breath. "I'll leave with Cody in the morning. Maybe you're right. Maybe I don't belong here anymore. Maybe I never did."

Turning around was almost the hardest thing she ever did. Walking out of his room, out of his life, nearly killed her.

Chapter Thirty-One

Jasmine didn't sleep. She stayed up to pack, and the rest of the time she spent worrying over her imminent departure. The idea of leaving Sweetwater scared her. It had been her haven, her sanctuary, for six years. Even when she'd lived in Paris, she'd known that this was home, that she would always be safe here.

Now she was poised to leave. This time for good. She would embrace a new family, strangers to her. The idea nearly sent her into full-fledged panic.

She waited until six-thirty, and then she went down the hall to knock on Cody's door. When she heard his call to come in, she opened the door and hesitantly eased inside.

He'd obviously just come from the bathroom. His hair was wet from a recent shower, and he was wiping his face as if he'd just shaved.

"Jasmine, hello. You're up early."

He looked surprised but happy by her intrusion.

She approached him nervously but still maintained her distance. He sat down on his bed and patted the space beside him. She stared for a moment then sat down.

"If your offer still stands, I'd like to leave with you," she said.

"Of course it's still open," he said gently. "Jasmine, I meant every word. Tara is very anxious to meet you. And I'd love the opportunity to spend time with you. Catch up on the last six years and hopefully make up for the time we lost."

"I'd want to leave today. This morning," she blurted out.

He blinked in surprise. "We can leave whenever you like, but are you sure?"

She nodded. "I'm sure."

"Okay. I only need a few minutes to get my stuff together. We can leave just as soon as you want."

Her chest squeezed with pain at the idea of leaving, and yet she knew she didn't have a choice. She couldn't stay.

"I'll meet you downstairs then. I need to bring my things down, and I want to say goodbye to Zane and Carmen."

"And not to Seth?" he asked gently.

She swallowed painfully. "I've already said my goodbyes to Seth."

"Leave your things in your room. I'll bring them down for you," he offered. "You go and have your time with Carmen and Zane."

She leaned forward and hugged him, albeit awkwardly. He seemed surprised but pleased by her overture. She pulled away abruptly and stood, anxious to be away.

"I'll see you downstairs," she said as she hurried for the door.

She went in search of Carmen, and when she found her, she couldn't even get the words out. Carmen held her close, stroking her hair as she shed torrents of tears.

"*Mi niña*, I will miss you so," Carmen choked out. "You are truly the daughter of my heart. Swear to me that you will call."

"I love you, *mamacita*," Jasmine said as emotion grew thicker in her throat.

"*Te amo, mi niña, te amo.*"

"You're going," Zane said quietly.

Jasmine wrenched herself from Carmen's arms and turned to see Zane standing in the doorway to the kitchen. His eyes were hooded and wary, his entire stance tense.

Carmen gave her a little push. "Go on, *niña*," she whispered. "He is hurting too."

Jasmine walked like a jerky puppet across the kitchen floor until she came to a stop in front of Zane. He yanked her to him, hugging her close. His heart beat in a frantic cacophony against her cheek.

When she finally pulled away, there were tears in both their eyes.

"Please understand, Zane. I can't stay here. Not when...not when he's here. It wouldn't be fair to any of us."

"I love you, Jaz. I'm not letting you go so easily."

She tried to smile, but she faltered. She sucked in her breath, determined not to break down. "Give me time, Zane. I need some time to figure this all out. I love you so much. I've made such a mess of things, and now I have to straighten it out."

Zane slid his hand down her hair and then over her cheek. "I'm not giving up on us. You take your time. You think about what it is you want, what you need. And then I'm coming for you, Jaz."

He pulled her to him in a long, breathless kiss. So much sadness welled between them. It was tender, heartbreaking, a goodbye that neither of them wanted to say.

Cody cleared his throat. "I'm ready when you are, Jasmine. I've loaded your stuff into the truck. Take as long as you need. I'll wait for you outside."

Jasmine pulled away from Zane's lips and laid her forehead on his chest. Her fingers dug into his waist, and she held on for dear life. Never had she thought she'd be leaving like this.

"I love you," she whispered.

Zane held her close and kissed the top of her head. "I know you're hurting right now, Jaz. And that you need time to get over your hurt. But know that I love you. I'll always love you."

She closed her eyes, pressed her forehead a little closer into his chest, and then she pushed away, wiping her eyes with the back of her hand.

"I should go. I don't want to keep him waiting," she croaked.

Carmen and Zane walked with her outside and watched as Cody ushered her into his truck. As they began to pull away, Jasmine gave a half-hearted wave as she saw Zane pull Carmen into a hug.

All the way down the winding driveway of the ranch, she stared out the back window. Her home. Her one safe place. So beautiful. So full of love and warmth. She was leaving, and she'd probably never be back.

Her nose stung, and she swallowed back tears even as they gathered in her eyes, making her beloved landscape swim in her vision. As she let her gaze pan out from the ranch, there on a hillside, silhouetted by the early morning sun, was a huge buck. Old Man. He stood staring at her as she stared at him, and then he turned and bolted away, disappearing over the next rise.

She bowed her head and cried.

Chapter Thirty-Two

"You look like one screwed-up mother fucker."

Seth scowled and looked up as J.T. sat beside him at the bar. "Gee thanks, I needed that."

J.T. shrugged. "That's what friends are for." He sat down and motioned to the bartender for a beer. He glanced sideways at Seth. "So how's Jasmine?"

Seth closed his eyes and rubbed his forehead with his hand. "Gone."

"Gone? What the hell? Where's she gone?"

"She went to stay with her brother," Seth said bleakly.

He opened his eyes to see J.T. staring at him, an odd expression on his face. "Why did she go?"

Seth looked straight ahead again. "Because I didn't ask her to stay."

"Uh huh. Any particular reason you didn't ask her to stay?"

"She loves Zane."

"Uh huh."

"Zane loves her."

"Yeah."

"She says she loves me."

Seth waited but all he got from J.T. was silence. He turned to stare at his friend but found only bland disinterest on his face.

"You don't think that's fucked up?"

J.T. shrugged again, a gesture that was fast getting on Seth's nerves. "I don't figure it's any of my business."

Seth blew out his breath in frustration. Beside him J.T. continued to sip at his beer, but then nothing much bothered J.T. A more laid-back bastard you wouldn't find. The minutes ticked by and then out of the blue, "Do you love her?"

Seth turned sharply. "It's not that simple."

"Yeah, man, it is," J.T. said calmly. "Do you love her?"

Seth felt his composure start to crack. "I've always loved her."

"Then what's the problem?"

"I think you must have been dropped on your head too many times as a baby," Seth muttered. "The problem is self-evident. I'm in love with a woman who also loves my brother and who wants...us both."

"And you don't want to share her."

The answer should have come immediately, but he sat there, the words difficult to form. "I'm not sure I can."

"So you're not vehemently opposed in theory."

"You sound way too rational about this," Seth said in irritation.

J.T. shrugged yet again. "One of us has to be. It seems pretty simple in my book. You love her. She loves you. I'm assuming Zane doesn't have a problem because I don't see him here drowning his sorrows in cheap-ass beer. You've probably both had sex with her."

Seth glared at J.T. "And just how the fuck would you know that?"

"Dude, I'm the one who lent her the handcuffs. I doubt she would have had to fight Zane much to get him into her bed. That only leaves you."

"You're a twisted mother fucker," Seth muttered.

"Yeah, well, I'm not the one who pushed away a woman I've loved forever, and in the process made not only me but my brother miserable, not to mention that little girl who's probably off crying her eyes out somewhere."

"We are so not having this conversation."

J.T. stood and tossed a few bills onto the bar. "I've got to run. Early shift tomorrow. But if you want my unsolicited advice? Pull your head out of your ass before you fuck up the best thing that's ever happened to you and to Zane. If your choices are living without her, which clearly isn't working out for you, or sharing her with another man who loves her as deeply as you do, then the answer seems pretty damn clear to me."

He walked away, leaving Seth there to curse him. He made it sound so simple. It could never be that simple. Could it?

∛

Jasmine sat in her brother's living room, playing with her nephew. He was just starting to pull up and stand, and he delighted in mauling Jasmine with sloppy baby kisses.

It had been a week since they'd returned to Louisiana. Cody and Tara both had done everything in their power to make Jasmine feel comfortable and at home, but she was grieving for the family and home she'd left behind in Texas.

She couldn't stay here forever. The idea of depending on her brother and sister-in-law to provide for her didn't sit well. She had skills. She had a job offer with *Wildscapes*. She just had to buck up the courage to take it.

"Jasmine," Tara said as she entered the living room, "would you like to go out to eat with us? Cody just called from the jobsite, and he's running a little late so he wanted to know if we'd meet him for dinner."

Jasmine shook her head. "You guys go on without me. Would you like me to watch Thomas for you so you two can eat alone?"

Tara smiled. "You're very sweet, Jasmine, but you've watched him all week. If I had any more time alone, I'd think I was childless. You should get out. You've been holed up in this house ever since you got here."

Jasmine shrugged uncomfortably. How could she go out and have fun when she felt dead on the inside?

Tara knelt down in front of her and collected Thomas as he set to climbing Jasmine's shoulder again. "Jasmine, I know you're hurting," she said kindly. "Cody and I are worried about you. We want you to be happy."

Jasmine smiled but felt like it might well crack her face. "I'll be all right," she lied. Well, it could be the truth. Eventually she would be. One day.

Tara sighed and stood with Thomas gurgling in her arms. "I'll see you later then. Be sure and eat something, okay?"

Jasmine nodded and watched as she walked away, babbling nonsense to her baby. An evening alone sounded heavenly. Tara and Cody had smothered her since her arrival. They meant well, but Jasmine was ready to scream. She just wanted a few moments where she could be alone with her misery. Close her eyes and just be alone.

She had a lot of decisions to make. For a short time, she'd allowed herself to believe that she just might be able to have a future with the two men she loved with every piece of her soul. Now that her dream had shattered in tiny, jagged pieces, it was time to pull herself together and dream about something else. If only she could.

ℂ

"I'm worried as hell about her," Cody said.

Zane swore and held the phone closer to his ear.

"She's not eating. I doubt she's sleeping. She's lost weight, and she just looks so damn unhappy."

Zane closed his eyes and rubbed the back of his neck with his free hand. "Thanks for calling me, man. I appreciate it."

"I don't give a damn if you appreciate it," Cody exploded. "I want to know if you're going to do something about it."

"Yeah," Zane said. "I am."

He hung the phone up, his mind already made up. It had been made up the day Jaz left the ranch with Cody, but Zane had promised her time. Well, fuck that. She'd had enough time, and according to Cody, she was wasting away.

He went in search of Seth with a sense of purpose beating a steady rhythm. Things had sucked with a capital "S" ever since Jaz had left. Carmen walked around in tears, her eyes and nose puffy and red. She hadn't cooked a meal in a week, and her kitchen was in shambles. Zane had avoided Seth and brooded in silence, and Seth, well, the few times Zane had seen him, had acted surly and pissed off. And that was his own fucking fault.

A sense of peace he wasn't expecting fell over him as he sought out his brother. For as long as he could remember, his life had been entrenched in this ranch, in their business. It should panic him that he was breaking away, wanting a life with Jaz away from everything that was familiar to them both. But instead, he felt relief that he'd be with the woman he loved.

He found Seth in the barn grooming Jaz's horse. He almost turned and walked away because Seth's face was locked in stone. But the longer he put it off, the longer he was without Jaz, and that was not an option.

"I'm leaving," he said then cringed at how bluntly it came out.

Seth stopped what he was doing and turned to stare at Zane. Zane almost felt sorry for the bastard. Almost.

"What do you mean?" Seth asked.

"I'm going after Jaz," he said in an easier tone. "I love her. Living here...is not an option for us so I'll go where she is. I want her, even if it means only having a part of her heart."

Pain glittered brightly in Seth's eyes. His jaw worked up and down, and he seemed to struggle with what he wanted to say.

"I understand," he said quietly. "But Zane, the ranch is your home."

"It was Jaz's too," Zane said simply. "It's been hers since we brought her here six years ago. I've never envisioned a future here that didn't include her. I understand why she can't be here, but I can't live without her, so if that means leaving, then I'm prepared to do that."

"How can you be so accepting of what she wants?" Seth asked in a strangled voice.

Zane looked him calmly in the eye. "I don't know a lot about love or what it's supposed to mean. I don't know how it works for other people. I don't really care. What I do know, is that I love her. And that means my love doesn't come with a set of conditions. Does it bother me to know she loves you and probably always will? No. Because she loves me, too. I'm not threatened by that because I know she'd never do anything to hurt me. Could I share her with you? If my choices were having her whole and happy, sparkling and sharing her with you; or having a part of her, knowing she'd never completely shine and be whole but having her all to myself, then I wouldn't even have to think about it. Because loving her means I want her happy. I want the best for her. I don't ever want to have any part in making her sad."

Seth looked stunned by all that Zane had said. Zane, however felt as though a great weight had lifted from him. Yeah, he was making the right decision.

"I'm going to pack," he said softly, and he turned to walk away, anticipation tightening every muscle.

Chapter Thirty-Three

Seth stood outside Zane's door listening to his brother throw his clothes into a suitcase. His family was crumbling around him, and only he had the power to stop it. He had to have the courage to take a chance.

It terrified him and gave him hope all at the same time. Could it really be as simple as trusting himself and trusting Jasmine? Could a relationship between the three of them work? No more guilt, no more angst, just an embracing of something different and yet so special?

He pushed the door open wider and stepped inside. Zane looked up and paused in the zipping of his suitcase.

"Tell me something, Zane. I need to know the truth. Are you really okay with the idea of sharing Jasmine...with me?"

Zane straightened his stance, his expression serious. "I won't lie to you, man. In the beginning I was jealous. But it seemed natural that she'd love you, too. The only fear I've ever had is being the lower rung on the ladder. Assuming the role of the younger brother, not considered an equal. I love Jasmine just as much as you do, and I assume just as much responsibility for her and her happiness."

Seth nodded. "I understand. I'd never want you to feel second best, not when it's the fear I hold most. I realized something after Jasmine left."

"Yeah, what's that?" Zane asked, his voice cautious.

Seth let go of the door and shut it behind him. "I realized I wasn't allowing myself to trust Jasmine. That the whole time she was telling me she loved me just as much as you, I didn't believe her. And maybe, for this to work, I have to be willing to have faith in her. Believe in her."

Zane nodded.

"It won't be easy, and maybe that'll be my fault, but I want to try, Zane. I don't want to live without her. I don't want you to leave here. I want to bring her home. To us."

An expression of pure relief flooded Zane's face. He sat down on the bed, his hands trembling. "Are you sure?"

"I'm not sure of anything but the fact that I love her and that we're both miserable without her. There has to be a way to make this work, and I want to find it."

Zane smiled then, and Seth realized that he hadn't smiled since Jasmine had left. None of them had.

"Maybe you should go get packed," Zane said, "because I plan to leave in the next thirty minutes."

ॐ

Jasmine was just finishing dinner with her brother and sister-in-law when the doorbell rang. Cody excused himself to go answer the door while she and Tara began clearing the table.

"I'm glad to see you eating better," Tara said as she walked around Jasmine with a pile of plates.

"I've missed Cajun food," she replied. "Carmen cooks some mean Tex-Mex and Mexican food, but I haven't had Cajun food since Mama used to cook her etoufee."

"I hope mine measures up," Tara said with a grin.

"It was terrific."

Both women looked up when Cody walked back into the kitchen, a smile on his face. He dropped a kiss on his wife's lips then turned to Jasmine, eyes gleaming.

"There's someone here to see you."

Jasmine blinked in surprise.

"In the living room."

She stared between her brother and Tara, who now wore a wide smile of her own.

"Go on," Tara encouraged. "Cody can help me finish up."

Jasmine turned and walked on stiff legs into the living room. When she saw both Zane *and* Seth standing there, her mouth fell open in shock.

"What are you doing here?" she whispered.

"We've come to take you home," Seth said gruffly.

Her heart pounded furiously. There was only one way she'd return to Sweetwater, only one condition. He had to know that. To give her false hope was terribly cruel.

She wiped her hands down her jeans, unsure of what to say. Too afraid to give voice to her hopes. All she could do was stare, so hungrily.

Seth and Zane both moved toward her, their expressions softening with something that looked so much like love. They each took a hand and guided her toward the couch to sit.

"Cody was right," Zane said grimly. "You look like hell."

Her gaze shot to his, her hopes sinking fast. "Is that why you're here?" she asked dully. "Because Cody was worried about me?"

"No," Seth said, turning her chin toward him. "We're here because we love you, and we want you to come home."

Her eyes widened.

"Yes, Jasmine, you heard right. We love you. We want you to come home. We want you with us always."

She glanced between Zane and Seth but if she thought to find doubt or disagreement between them, she found only calm acceptance.

"You changed your mind?" she said in wonderment.

"I think Zane's has always been made up," Seth said ruefully. "I was the hard-headed bastard. And I'm sorry that I hurt you so many times. I won't hurt you again, Jasmine. I want this to work. I'm willing to do what it takes to make it work."

She threw her arms around Seth's neck and held him as tight as she could. Then she turned and did the same to Zane. She was in sensory overload. She wanted to crawl all over both of them, hugging, touching and kissing them. Finally she settled for pulling them close to her sides so she was held firmly between them.

"Zane?" she asked, looking up at him.

He put a gentle finger to her lips. "We've talked, Jaz. We can do this. Seth and I are good, I promise."

The tears she'd been trying so valiantly to hold at bay trickled down her cheeks. And then more came and soon she was sobbing great big noisy sobs as each man held her, stroking her and murmuring soothing words.

"I thought this would make you happy," Seth said with a chuckle. "We didn't come all this way to make you cry."

She kissed him, cupping his face in her hands. "I am happy. So happy." And then she started crying again.

Zane laughed and pulled her onto his lap. "You have to stop, Jaz." He squeezed her to him and pulled her hair away from her face.

She buried her face in his neck and clung to him, so very afraid this was all the product of too many sleepless nights and that she'd finally fallen asleep only to dream wonderful, impossible dreams.

"I thought I'd lost any chance I ever had of making you both love me," she whispered. "I made so many mistakes. I handled things all wrong, and still, you're here. I cannot even begin to tell you how completely and wonderfully happy I am right now."

Zane pressed his lips to her hair, and Seth reached out to take her hand.

"Will you come back home with us, Jasmine?" Seth asked. "I promised Carmen before we left that we'd return her family to her. But more than that, I promised myself to bring back the one person who ties us all together. You."

She reached out to touch his face. He nuzzled into her palm then reached up to take her hand, turning it over to kiss the soft pad of her thumb.

"Yes, Seth. Please take me back. Take me home."

Epilogue

She entered the water with barely a ripple. Jasmine skimmed along the bottom of the pool, her arms fanning out as she propelled herself forward.

The water surrounded her, sliding sensuously over her body, and she felt light, at ease. She closed her eyes and enjoyed the cool caress over her bare skin. Here, she felt weightless, like she was flying.

Her chest tightened as she felt the twinges of her lungs, starved for oxygen. Almost reluctantly, she pushed herself upward, breaking the surface of the water. She sucked in a mouthful of air as her hands gripped the side of the pool.

When she opened her eyes, she saw a worn set of boots mere inches from her fingers. She looked up just as Seth squatted. He reached for her and pulled her from the pool and into his arms as he stood.

"I'm going to get you wet," she murmured just as he closed his lips over hers.

"I don't care," he murmured back.

She melted into him. Her arms twined around his neck as he deepened his kiss. She let out a long sigh of contentment when he moved from her lips to her jaw and finally down the curve of her neck.

When he nibbled a path toward her breast, she grinned but made no effort to push him away.

"I've always wanted to fuck in the pool," he said. He nuzzled aside her bikini top then ran his tongue over one taut nipple.

She groaned and arched more fully into his mouth. "You're not dressed for swimming."

She felt his lips turn upwards.

"Who said anything about being dressed?"

"My thoughts exactly," she said.

Over the last year, her battle with the swimming pool would best be described as volatile. It hadn't been easy, and it hadn't been overnight, but Seth and Zane had been patient with her and never tried to push her before she was ready.

Now swimming was nearly a daily ritual. The water that had long been such an enemy was now one of her greatest indulgences.

As Seth tugged on the strings of her bikini, she grabbed for his shirt. She wasn't careful, didn't care if she ripped the damn thing.

Seth had her naked before she managed to get his shirt off, and with a growl of impatience, he stepped back to hastily do the job himself. He yanked his jeans down his hips and kicked them, along with the boots he'd shucked, toward one of the chairs.

She smiled, gave him her best come-hither look and crooked her finger. He paced forward, a lean, hungry look simmering in his eyes. She backed away and hopped over the side of the pool.

She landed with a splash, got her footing then glanced up to where he stood. "Come and get me," she challenged.

He quirked one brow, and she being the smart girl she was, turned and dove under the water, heading as quick as she could into deeper water.

She didn't get far.

A strong arm closed around her waist, and she surged upward as Seth yanked them both to the surface. His mouth was on hers almost before she could take a breath.

He picked her up and stalked through the shallow end until her back met the hard edge of the pool.

"Put your legs around my waist," he rasped.

When she complied, he cupped her ass, spreading her. One hand left her, and he reached between them to position his cock at her pussy entrance.

He thrust hard. Their coming together was urgent and hurried. She wrapped her arms around his neck and held on as he fucked her against the side of the pool.

"I'm a married woman. I shouldn't be doing stuff like this," she teased.

He buried himself in her and took several long, shuddering breaths close to her ear. "Yes, but fucking my brother's wife has such a forbidden quality to it, don't you think?"

She sank her teeth into his neck and nipped him in retaliation.

"Ouch. Damn it, woman."

A year ago, Jasmine wouldn't have taken such a statement so lightly, but then Seth wouldn't have made a joke of it either. When their relationship was in its infancy and the three struggled to forge a tenuous bond, Seth had suggested that Zane be the one to legally marry Jasmine.

Her heart softened all over again when she thought of how hard it must have been for Seth to make that offer. But he hadn't wanted Zane to think he would ever take a backseat in the relationship.

So she and Zane had been married in J.T.'s office by the local judge. Then Seth and Zane had whisked her off to Paris for a honeymoon. Cherisse arranged a ceremony where Jasmine was wed to Seth and promised to both men. It had been beautiful, emotional and it was a night she'd never forget.

"It's a damn big insult for a woman to leave the building when a man's making love to her," Seth said dryly.

She reached up to touch his face. "I was remembering Paris."

His blue eyes sparked, and he kissed her hungrily. He eased forward again, and the cool water splashed up her sides. His arms tightened around her, his mouth fused hotly to hers as his hips met her flesh again and again.

A low moan tore from her throat as his mouth fed hungrily on her. His lips glanced down her neck and to the soft spot under her ear. She threw back her head and gave herself over to the pleasure he lavished on her.

The sun warmed her face, but Seth's love warmed her heart.

He shuddered against her as her orgasm broke and splintered through her body. For a long moment, he held her there, buried between her legs, his taut muscles coiling beneath her fingertips.

"God, I love you," he said raggedly.

"Carmen will be home soon," she whispered. "And I love you, too."

He pulled away and smiled. Bereft of his closeness, the water quickly chilled around her, and she shivered. He picked her up and waded to the steps.

Water fell from their bodies and splattered the concrete as he headed for the kitchen door.

"Carmen's going to kill us if we get her floors wet," Jasmine muttered.

Seth set her down inside the door. "Wait here and I'll get us some towels."

She rubbed her hands up and down her arms and bounced on her toes in order to keep warm as he dashed naked up the stairs. Seconds later, he enveloped her in a towel and dried her from head to toe.

He leaned down to kiss her. "Get upstairs and get some clothes on or Carmen will scold me for not taking better care of you."

Jasmine snorted. "As if."

But she hurried up anyway to shower and dress. Anticipation curled in her stomach when she glanced at the clock. In just a few more hours Zane would be home.

છ

Seth watched Jasmine yawn and battle sleep as she struggled to remain focused on the movie they were watching. She glanced at the clock every few minutes, and he knew she was anxious for Zane to get home.

He smiled and shook his head. He should be out of his mind with jealousy but a year into his very unique relationship with Jasmine, he'd mellowed a whole hell of a lot. Learning to share the woman he loved with another man who loved her just as much—well, it hadn't been easy. There were still times he could get mighty possessive, but for the most part, he'd learned to chill the fuck out.

He grinned when he saw her head meet the arm of the couch. So much for staying up for Zane.

Half an hour later, he heard the front door open. He looked up to see Zane walk in and drop his suitcase on the floor. Seth held a finger to his lips then motioned to the couch where Jasmine was sleeping.

Zane's eyes lit up, and the fatigue that seemed etched on his brother's face lifted and fell away as he looked at Jasmine.

"How was the trip?" Seth asked in a low voice.

"Good, but I'm damn glad to be home."

"Jasmine tried to stay up for you," Seth said with a hint of laughter. "She crapped out about thirty minutes ago."

Zane smiled but Seth could see the hunger in his eyes. He got out of the recliner and pointed the remote at the TV to turn it off. "I'm going to head on up to bed. You should wake her and tell her you're home. She's really missed you."

"Yeah, sure. We'll be up in a while then," Zane said.

Seth turned toward the stairs even as Zane walked to the couch and knelt in front of it. Jasmine opened her eyes, and he watched the joy that filled them when she saw Zane. Then her gaze found Seth, and he saw the same love reflected there for him. His chest tightened, and an odd sort of fulfillment settled around his heart.

This was right. Their love was right.

He headed up the stairs, determined to give Zane and Jasmine some privacy. He cherished his own moments alone with her, and he wouldn't deprive his brother of the same.

Later when Zane carried Jasmine into the big bedroom they'd remodeled to accommodate the three of them, they both made love to her. And she showed them again, as she had so many times before, that there was room in her heart for both of them.

About the Author

Maya Banks is the pen name for Sharon Long, who writes for Samhain under both names. She lives in Texas with her husband, three children and assortment of cats. When she's not writing, she can be found hunting, fishing or playing poker. A southern girl born and bred, Maya loves life below the Mason Dixon, and more importantly, loves bringing southern characters and settings to life in her stories.

To learn more about Maya, please visit www.mayabanks.com. Send an email to Maya at maya@mayabanks.com or join her Yahoo! group to join in the fun with other readers as well as Maya: http://groups.yahoo.com/group/writeminded_readers.

One island...One woman...Two studs

Stranded
© *2007 Eve Vaughn*

India Powers is at the end of her rope. After dumping her cheating fiancé and having a falling out with her parents, she decides to take a much needed vacation. In route she meets two hunky fellow vacationers in the form of Rafe Santiago and Grant Thompson. Though she's not looking for love, India sees no harm in a little island flirtation.

Rafe and Grant have been friends since they were kids; both from broken homes, all they had were each other. Their closeness leads them to the discovery they enjoy sharing the same women. After surviving a stormy marriage that nearly destroys their friendship, Rafe vows to never let another woman come between them. To celebrate Rafe's divorce, he and Grant take a vacation in hopes of finding Miss Right along the way.

Tragedy strikes when their plane goes down. In a twist of fate, the only survivors are India, Grant and Rafe. Stranded for weeks, their daily fight for survival turns into something much deeper when India falls for both men and they for her. However, when they're rescued and returned to civilization, they fall under public scrutiny. Can their newfound love survive when outside forces step in to tear them apart?

Available now in ebook and print from Samhain Publishing.

hot stuff

Discover Samhain!
THE HOTTEST NEW PUBLISHER ON THE PLANET

Romance, fantasy, mystery, thriller, mainstream and
more—Samhain has more selection, hotter authors, and
everything's available in both ebook and print.

Pick your favorite, sit back, and enjoy the ride!
Hot stuff indeed.

GREAT
cheap
fun

Discover eBooks!

THE FASTEST WAY TO GET THE HOTTEST NAMES

Get your favorite authors on your favorite reader, long before they're
out in print! Ebooks from Samhain go wherever you go, and work with
whatever you carry—Palm, PDF, Mobi, and more.

WWW.SAMHAINPUBLISHING.COM